Lost or Strayed, One U.N.C.L.E. Agent

Their assignment seemed deceptively easy: to find out why THRUSH and the countess from Corfu were interested in stealing a harmless communicator module the army had developed. That is, it seemed simple until Waverly told Solo and Kuryakin about Frank Stanton.

"Mr. Stanton went to Corfu seven months ago, gentlemen. I heard from him just once, to let me know he had arrived safely. Since then . . . nothing!"

The room was silent as the two agents digested this fact.

Waverly went on: "In the last raid, one man was hit; he and his car were subsequently burned beyond recognition. But his recovered gun, and the prints on it, belong to our man, Frank Stanton! And he was working *with* THRUSH, gentlemen!"

Even then Solo and Illya couldn't have guessed what a strange and dangerous assignment they faced . . . but they were soon to find out!

This is the twentieth in Ace Books' series of exciting MAN FROM U.N.C.L.E. novels. For information on earlier books, see pages 157 and 158.

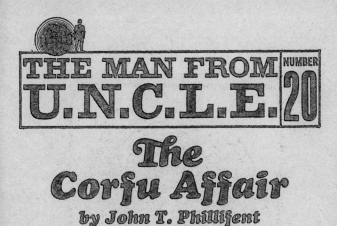

THE MAN FROM U.N.C.L.E.

NUMBER 20

The Corfu Affair

by John T. Phillifent

AN ACE BOOK

Ace Publishing Corporation
1120 Avenue of the Americas
New York, N.Y. 10036

THE CORFU AFFAIR

Printed in U.S.A.

CHAPTER ONE

TROOPER DAVIS stared at the high-wire fence and yawned, glanced at the luminous dial of his wristwatch, yawned again, and smothered a groan. Only twelve-thirty and already he felt as if he had been awake for half the night. It was a nice night, and warm, but all the same he would rather have been in the sack. He marched a pace or two, felt the butt of his slung rifle beating gently against his rump, heard the crunch of gravel under his own feet, and smiled at himself. This tour of duty was a snap. He grumbled purely as reflex. There were worse places to be. Vietnam, for instance.

All the same, who wants to be awake and alert when everyone else is snoring? And for what? He glanced enviously at the guard shack, then let his gaze travel back to the dark blockhouses back there. A Research Center. He mouthed it with faint scorn. Had it been missiles, now, or nuclear energy stuff, something like that—but who in his right mind was going to break into a place like this? To steal radio spares? From what little he knew of radio hams, they were the least likely people to be militant. He had half-turned away with a shrug when just the flicker of a fugitive light caught the corner of his eye.

He froze, then slowly turned to stare fixedly, not daring to look away in case he missed the flash again.

Imagination? No, damn it, there it went again, a flitting spot from a tight beam. And it was where no light ought to be, on the inside of one of those dark windows. All his scorn gone in a breath, Davis shrugged his rifle from his shoulder into his ready hands and ran to the guard shack. The sergeant of the guard came awake with a grunt. Two snorts later he was on his feet.

"What?"

"Intruders in Block B. I saw a light."

"Get back out there and stay with it!" The sergeant hit the light switch and raised his voice harshly. "Guard detail up! On your feet! Come on, snap it up!" Without waiting for responses he plunged out of the shack and ran to join the sentry. "Where? Show me!"

There was no need for words. As Davis pointed the light twinkled again, moving, at the window this time.

"They're on the way out," the sergeant growled, then raised his voice again. "Halt! Stand fast or we fire!"

As fast as an echo came the spit and crack of a shot. Davis heard his sergeant go down with a gasping grunt. He dropped to a knee, aimed and fired at the dancing light—one—two—three times, and the crash of his fusillade put wings to the feet of the hastening guard detail. Light flared, to reveal two dark-clad figures sprinting crazily for the far corner of the fence, where they went headlong through a hole already prepared, and disappeared. The sentry ran heavily, cursing as he heard a car engine start up, fired twice more in despair, and then halted at the fence as he heard an engine revving into speed and then dwindling away fast. Seconds later he heard the guard jeep stutter into life and go snarling past in pursuit, with three men on the jump to get aboard.

6

Voices broke out in bitter questions. Davis turned away and ran, then halted as he heard yet another engine break into a roar and go away. That one sounded like a motorcycle. He shrugged and ran on to where the wounded man was struggling to sit up, cursing savagely. Brass-bound authority infiltrated the scene. Questions and more questions. Medical aid for the sergeant, hit badly but with a good chance of survival. There was the open window to be checked, then the interior. Within half an hour civilian experts had been rousted from their beds and were on the spot examining the outrage. Fifteen minutes later saw the return of the guard jeep with a grim story. They had given the runaway a hard chase. Knowing that the sergeant was hit they had not hesitated to use whatever weapons they had to incite the fugitives to halt. In the end they had forced the fleeing car off the road, over a high cutbank, and it was now lying at the foot of a rocky gorge some ten miles away, blazing furiously.

The driver-corporal reported: "I posted one man to stand by so that we could get back here fast, report, and get help. Not a prayer of getting the bodies out of that car. It's a total write-off, but anyway, we stopped 'em!"

The sentry now reported the second noise he had heard—of the motorcycle—and the civilian experts looked savage.

"Window forced clean, alarms cut, fence cut. They knew what they were after and they got them. A whole gross of units, and one man could stuff them in a pocket easily. That's the second time in a year! God only knows what they want those units for, but they've got them!"

And so the matter moved into the spheres of higher authority.

Alexander Waverly was peevish. It was not unusual for Number One, Section One, of the United Network Command for Law and Enforcement, to show irritation on occasion, or even a dash of mild wrath, but this was different. He was being openly irritable in the presence of guests. Both Napoleon Solo and Illya Nikovetch Kuryakin knew the old man's habits well enough to be able to discern this novelty immediately. They found seats and stood by while Waverly made introductions, wondering just what was biting the old man.

"General Hagen is head of the army's technical research committee. Sergeant Alison Rowland is his aide. And this is Dr. Luther de Wet, the Director of Research at Fort Westaway. Now—it really is astonishing that in an organization such as ours, dedicated to efficiency in all directions, it is apparently impossible to obtain a respectable cup of coffee. Please accept my apologies." Waverly made a gesture to his guests. "One can only presume that the qualifications for exercising control over crime do not coincide with an ability to cook. The canteen service is deplorable!"

"I'm sure, sir," Solo murmured, "you haven't brought these distinguished people here just to discuss food!"

"That's all right!" General Hagen patted the air with a pacifying hand. "We've had a lot worse lunches than that, Waverly. You should have to live on army grub sometime. I take it you want me to put these men in the picture?"

"And myself," Waverly said. "I've only the outline sketch so far."

"All right. I can give you facts, things that have happened. I can't give you reasons, because I don't have them. This whole business is cockeyed. Show them the sample, Alison."

Miss Rowland unzipped a neat leather case and produced a small clear-plastic bag which she handed first to Waverly.

"We call that a module-pair," Hagen went on. "Tell 'em what it's for, Alison."

Miss Rowland sat again, composed herself, and said: "The two objects you see are a perfect match for each other. They are solid-state modules which are, in themselves, complete radio-circuits. Attached to suitable amplifying equipment, they serve as two-way radio-communication units of very small size. The only remarkable thing about them in practice, apart from the small size, is that they are extremely critical on frequency. The pair will resonate in harmony with each other, but not to any other wave-length except the precise one they are tuned to. In use, one module is mounted in a multiple control unit, the other in a trooper's equipment. He usually has it taped to his jaw, or behind the ear, leaving his hands free. The result is that one field-commander in the field can talk to any one of a squad of up to twenty men and hear replies. Or the commander can talk to all and hear all, of course, although that is not usually done."

Solo looked at the tiny objects before passing the bag to Kuryakin, who peered closely and saw two small silvery objects, each half an inch long and the size of a pencil-lead in thickness.

"A technical advance," the Russian agent said, "but

hardly a matter for high-ranking military concern, surely?"

"I warned you it was cockeyed," Hagen said. "Luther, you tell 'em how much those things are worth, will you?"

Dr. de Wet cleared his throat, adjusted his glasses and smiled, but with bewilderment rather than mirth. "The modules are extremely difficult to make. They require vacuum diffusion and zone-melting techniques and a critical standard of performance. We discard about fifty percent as below standard. So, in that sense, they are valuable. Were it not a military project, the enterprise would not be worthwhile. But in themselves the modules are useless for anything but the intended purpose. It has been suggested that they might be sold to ham-radio people, but that is not a workable notion. One module is useless without the other or with some circuit precisely tuned to it. It would be like trying to sell a gross of keys, each of which will fit only one lock!"

"They aren't tunable?" Kuryakin asked, and the expert shook his head.

"Not at all. They are difficult to make, hard to replace, but of virtually no value. Why would anyone steal them?"

"That's where I take over," Hagen sat back and crossed one knee over the other. "About a year ago Westaway was broken into. Get the picture right, gentlemen. Fort Westaway is not exactly top security. Radio Research isn't like that. The raiders did more damage than anything else. They stole a few items, among which was a package containing a score, ten pairs, of those modules. As I say, they aren't secret, or precious, just of nuisance value to replace. Maybe a few soldiers will get killed who need not have done, and who cares about that?" Hagen's voice was bitter. "Of course, since the break-in we have posted a guard. For a year! And then, three days ago, repeat. Only this time the intruders knew exactly what to go for, and to get. And we think they got away. They took two packages this time. Nothing else, just two-score units, twenty matched pairs. The thieves were chased. They shot and almost killed the guard sergeant, so the troopers in pursuit weren't exactly tender. They ran a car off the road and the occupants were killed. The fire left practically nothing we could identify, except that we can say there were two people in the car—and a third who got clean away on a motorcycle. We might as well assume while we're at it that the third man got away with the modules. And there you have the situation. You have my word that nobody will break into Westaway again, but that's the well-known stable door routine. What we want to know is who, and why. Military Security is working on it, of course, but to be frank with you, it doesn't make sense. If this is the work of a foreign power or an enemy, we can't see it. I think it sounds like something in your line."

Half an hour later, after some questions had been asked and answered, the distinguished guests were conducted safely away, leaving Solo and Kuryakin to sit thoughtfully opposite Waverly.

"It's after the style of Thrush," Kuryakin said thoughtfully. "But I can't see what use those modules would be to anyone. I mean, they would make beautiful walkie-talkie outfits, but why break into a military establishment to steal them when you can make a fair substitute from any radio supplier? Unless there's something we have not been told?"

Waverly sighed. As a rule his appearance was that of an untidy and impractical scholar, a pedagogue setting his students some abstruse problem in delicate reasoning. Now he looked his age, a grim old man.

"We can set in motion the routine inquiries," he said, almost as if talking to himself. "We can increase the surveillance of Thrush laboratories and places of research in the hope that we will get some clue as to what they may intend to do with those modules. . . ."

"You're assuming it is Thrush, sir?"

"I am, Mr. Solo, and I will tell you why. But this is a matter to concern only the three of us, for the moment." That simple statement put a chill into the atmosphere of the room. A matter to be kept private to Waverly and his two top agents alone was something quite new in Solo's experience. He exchanged a glance with his colleague and saw the same tense expression of wonder reflected there.

"Allow me what may seem a digression, gentlemen." Waverly touched a switch and spun his chair so that he faced a screen. A picture came crisply into focus, a picture that made the two agents stare in amazement. In glorious color, it was a scene of rugged mountains raising their gray tips out of a mantle of olive green, with here and there scattered patches of a paler green, obviously walnut groves. Coastal cliffs edged the picture and a vivid blue sea sparkled in the foreground. But their eyes were drawn irresistibly to the fantastic stone pile that snuggled against those green slopes. The picture zoomed in suddenly, aiming at the building, and they saw that it was a palace, a towered and spired structure, colonnaded and battlemented, all in white stone and pink woodwork trim. It might have come direct from a Disney production.

A carefully impersonal voice began to recite: "This is the Argyr Palace," it said. "It stands on the island of Corfu some seven miles south of Corfu City. For many years untenanted and in decay, it was purchased some ten years ago by Countess Anne-Marie Louise de St-Denis and renovated. It is now her home for some eight months in every year."

The fairy-tale palace dissolved into a close-up of a face, still in color. "The Countess de St-Denis is thirty-four, of French-Italian descent, has been married four times, is now a widow, is owner and director-controller of the St-Denis Laboratories in Paris."

Solo stared and marveled. Belatedly he remembered that Corfu was Greek, and this was a face to make anyone remember. In some subtle way it failed to match the palace image. This woman was part Eve, part Aphrodite, with glossy black hair, vivid coloring on a flawless skin, eyes so blue as to be almost black, and a personal magnetism that radiated even from this, a mere picture. Yet, somehow, there was a touch of the Medusa about her too.

Waverly turned to look at his agents. "That woman," he said, "is the most dangerous person alive. That may sound like exaggeration, and I have never before said as much aloud for that very reason. But now I have evidence in proof of my statement. She is a brilliant brain, by any standards. From four marriages she has made money, gained skills, and is deeply involved with the higher council authorities of Thrush-Central. This much I know. In addition, she is a skillful cosmetic-surgeon in her own right and has a degree of earned fame in that field. But there's nothing she won't turn her hand to. The police and secret services of half a dozen nations would dearly love to be able to pin something on Countess Louise, and make it stick, but she is too clever for that. Take a good look, gentlemen, because we are going to move against her, and it's as well that you know just what you are taking on."

"Do we know anything factual about her, sir?" Kuryakin asked, and Solo echoed that in some wonder.

"I thought I was pretty well acquainted with the big villains of the world," he said. "And in particular the big guns in the Thrush hierarchy, but this lady is news to me."

"As I said"—Waverly nodded—"she is extremely clever. She is the power behind the throne always, never out in the open. Think of Corfu for a moment. It's a small island, not too easy to get at. Under Greek rule, a very uneasy government. Corfu City is the only settlement of any size, and it is little more than a town, only about thirty-five thousand people all told. For the rest—villages! Adequate surveillance is impossible in such a setup. Furthermore, the palace is accessible from the sea, so visitors can come and go virtually at will. Nevertheless I was able to learn that, about a year ago, the countess was entertaining guests, rather special guests. By twos and threes the top people in Thrush, the Hierarchy, were visiting her, very quietly and discreetly. There was a regular pattern, much too regular to be just coincidence."

"Any idea what's in the wind?"

"No idea at all, Mr. Solo. I wanted to know, of course; but remember what I said, Corfu is not easy to cover.

That is almost certainly why the countess chose it. In a place like that, one behaves like a tourist, or one sticks out like a sore thumb. I did not hope for quick and easy answers. But I did send a very good man to investigate."

"Anybody we know?"

"I think so, Mr. Kuryakin. You'd know him. Frank Stanton."

"They don't come any better," Solo said. "Frank gave me most of my basic training."

"And me," Kuryakin declared. "But surely he's a bit long in the tooth by now, sir. Due to come off the active list?"

Waverly sighed. "I sent Mr. Stanton to Corfu seven months ago, gentlemen. I heard from him just once, to let me know he had arrived safely. Since then—nothing!"

The room went silent as the two agents digested this fact. Then Solo stirred restlessly. "Frank could have made a slip," he suggested. "It's possible. A man has his off-days. I don't see that we have enough evidence, just on that, to move the countess up into the genius class. I'm sorry about Frank, but we all know the score when we go into a job. . . ."

"It's not that simple, Mr. Solo." Waverly moved the switch and shut off the Medusa face. "I had written off Mr. Stanton, with deep regret and the determination not to expose any other men to such a dangerous spot. I decided it was better to wait and see what devilish kind of brew the woman was hatching before trying again. But . . . well, look at these." He moved the switch again and now the screen held a picture showing a gun, a bullet, and several clear finger-and-palm prints.

"When General Hagen came to me for help he offered his fullest cooperation. This is part of it. His security people are very thorough. They lifted prints from the scene of the break-in. When the soldiers chased that getaway car they fired at it. They hit one man, causing him to drop a pistol. That man was subsequently burned beyond recognition in the car. The prints on the gun match those at the scene of the crime. The bullet which hit the sergeant was fired from that gun. Hagen admitted that he has not the facilities to trace either prints or gun. Nor has any agency he can call in. He gave them to us, to be of assistance. And they are. I've had them processed, because I thought I recognized the gun in any case. And I was right. That gun, and those prints, beyond any doubt, belong to Mr. Frank Stanton!"

Both men had seen this coming, but it was still a shock. Then Kuryakin spoke.

"Does the army know this?"

"No!" Waverly spoke quietly, but in his own way was more angry than either man had ever seen him before. "No one knows, except the three of us and the file-clerk who processed the prints, and even she doesn't know the background. I may be wrong, but I am of the opinion that the information would not help the army at all. What is left of Mr. Stanton is in that burned-out car, and that's the end of it, so far as they are concerned. For us it is a different matter. That is why I wish to confine it to us three, at the moment. If I'm to wash dirty linen, I prefer as small an audience as possible."

"You think Frank Stanton turned renegade?"

"It's a possibility we have to bear in mind. If he did, then he took a lot of very valuable information with him. If, on the other hand, that woman managed to bend him in some way, then we have to know how, and deal with it. Either way, this is an extremely delicate business."

"That's one assignment I want to volunteer for, sir. Frank taught me a lot." Solo said this very quietly. Kuryakin was just as quiet, and equally emphatic.

"Tell us what you have in mind," he said. "She won't bend us!"

"I expected nothing less," Waverly said. "But this is one case in which valor must give way to prudence. Never lose sight of this one fact. That woman is dangerous!"

CHAPTER TWO

Now THAT the bitter truth was out in the open Waverly seemed more like his usual pedantic self. Sitting back in his chair he surveyed his two men.

"Let me spell out the situation in detail," he said. "As I've already explained, Corfu is difficult. It is small, so that strangers tend to be conspicuous. We cannot possibly undertake an action in force unless and until we are absolutely sure of our ground. And we can hope for nothing from the local authorities. What's needed at the moment is information, a lot more information, before we can take any decisive action of any kind."

"The time of year is right," Solo offered. "What could be more natural than a tourist wanting to look over a palace?"

"I imagine that is precisely what Stanton thought," Waverly pointed out. "We can't go at it as easily as that. Above all, I must have your assurance that you will not initiate any action until you have obtained sufficient hard data."

Solo looked pained. "I'm not about to let her take my scalp, sir. It's not the thing for me to say, but I am not exactly strange to the ways of good-looking women."

"This woman is more than just a pretty face, Mr. Solo. She has buried four husbands already." Waverly swung his chair to face the impassive Russian agent.

"You, Mr. Kuryakin, will approach the other aspect

of the business. As you heard, Countess Louise is owner and director of a laboratory in Paris. The laboratory specializes in bio-chemicals, with special emphasis on cosmetic surgery. You will investigate that end. You will, if possible, get into the business."

"Any idea how, sir?"

"Yes. You'll have to look it up, but there is this. Surgery, and particularly orthopedic surgery, is increasingly involving itself with electronic aids. Heart pacemakers, artificial limb control, radar for the blind and so on. Familiarize yourself with the latest matters in that field. You will assume a suitable identity. You will go by a roundabout route into the U.S.S.R. We will have cooperation laid on. From there, after an adequate period to establish a background, you will enter Paris. You will be an undesirable Russian bio-electronics specialist seeking to do a shady deal with the St-Denis laboratories. And so on. We can elaborate that as we go along. For the beginning you need to get into the technicalities of that part. Understood?"

"If you say so, sir." Kuryakin shrugged and kept his reservations to himself. Studying up on electronic aids to surgery and similar fields would be no more than a chore, and he didn't mind that part. But entering the Soviet Union was something he didn't care for at all. His homeland had memories that he would just as soon have forgotten.

Waverly dismissed the two men with a gesture, hardly bothering to watch them go. None knew better than he just what hazards he was sending them into, but he had that faculty indispensable to any commander, of being able to dismiss a problem entirely once it had been dealt with. Almost before they had left the room he was leaning back and reviewing the next stage in his strategy. First there would have to be a stringent check on all U.N.C.L.E. security, to minimize any valuable hints Stanton might have given away. That would have to be done without letting too many people suspect that one of U.N.C.L.E.'s best men had gone sour. Then there was the need to get those sample modules to research, to try to find out what Thrush, and in particular, Countess Louise, could want them for.

Also, as his insulted digestion complained to him, there was the matter of the canteen to be looked into. Others called it "cafeteria," but he called it "canteen," and either way it left a lot to be desired!

Outside Waverly's door the two agents paused for a brief word before going their separate ways. Kuryakin was more serious than usual.

"Take no chances with the black widow, Napoleon," he advised. "She has forgotten more about the battle of the sexes than you'll ever know."

"I've never been afraid of a woman in my life, Illya, and I'm too old to start now," the other retorted.

"Corfu is quite a place too. Your titular ancestor fought a battle or two there, and lost. It's a bad place. In Homer's time it was called Phaeacia. Remember, Ulysses was washed ashore there, and got into a lot of trouble with a woman."

"You should change your name to Cassandra, old man. What can she do, carve me up?"

"Why not? She's a surgeon, too."

"All right, dig me out a couple of artificial legs, huh? Say, Illya, what do you suppose she wants those modules for?"

"I've no idea, but I'll wager it's for nothing healthy!"

As the airport bus trundled him into Corfu City, Solo settled himself diligently into his guise of a typical tourist. His fellow-travelers were few and unremarkable and he anticipated no difficulty in slipping away from them. In himself he had made no spectacular changes, apart from wearing a rather louder suit than he really cared for. His real disguise lay in his expression and attitude, in the naïve wide-eyed gape and stare. Not that this required any great effort, as the place warranted it.

There was that peculiar clearness in the air, the purity of color and tint, the freshness of everything, that is to be found nowhere else in the world. Artists have been known to come with the intention of painting such scenery, only to give up in despair because it already looks like a fresh picture. Out there in the bay, beyond the long narrow causeway, were a couple of mysterious islands, where the gaunt ruins of some old buildings lifted the tops of their bones above thick green cypress. And over there, across the sea that was the Ionian Strait, he saw mighty snowcapped mountains, the Epirus mountains. That was Albania, and the stretch of water between had seen its quota of bloody conflict over the centuries. Sea battles of Christian against Turk, Knight versus Infidel . . . History. The whole place reeked of it.

The hotel was a pleasant surprise. Not up to Hilton standards, maybe, but the Corfu Palace was reasonably clean, efficient, and the people spoke a kind of English good enough for him to understand. After inspecting and approving his room, and working the tourist image a bit more, he decided to quit wasting time. For all his apparent innocence, he was alert for any sign that anyone was taking more notice of him than was justified. He was not likely to forget what had happened to Frank Stanton, but he thought that if Countess Louise did have some kind of alarm system set for her, he might as well get out into the open and see how it worked. And it would help to do some reconnaissance of the land.

Accordingly, he slung a camera around his neck—only it wasn't a camera but an extremely powerful and compact telescope—and ventured out to explore the town. As he wandered through the narrow winding streets and pretended to be impressed by the Italian-style architecture, the gaudy shops, the unlovely apartment blocks, he kept alert for anyone appearing to be unduly curious in his doings, and at the same time tried to understand Stanton's method of work. The older man had been a quiet and effacing but very thorough worker, the type to take time to blend thoroughly with the scenery as a long-standing local resident. Judging purely by results, the approach had failed. Solo decided it might be just as well to throw away that pattern and try a different one. He would be the brash and obvious type, the man who has never been anywhere or seen anything before.

He saw no apparent hostility among the dark-tanned Corfiotes as he dutifully strolled the esplanade and admired the many bandstands, the view across the sparkling blue bay, the wealth of statues in the park, monuments to dead and gone British governors rather than those of the classical Greek kind, and the looming bulk of the old castle, standing up above the east end of the town. Because it was in character, he took time out to cast admiring glances on the many comely young women passing by. Here, as he saw, ancient and modern walked side by side. There were those who favored the traditional, and looked as if they might have just this minute stepped off the musical-comedy stage, with their gold-embroidered jackets in velvet over crisp white linen full-sleeved blouses; while others were as modern as any he might have seen back home, complete with mini-skirts and op-art prints.

It was warm. The constant tight-wound tension of trying to do several things at once while seeming to be doing nothing at all made him even warmer. In a while he selected an open-fronted cafe at random and waited for an attractive dark-eyed waitress to attend to him.

"Just something long and cool to drink," he told her, as soon as he discovered she could manage rudimentary English.

"Not food? You want to eat something too?"

"Not really, not unless it's just a light snack. You understand what I mean by 'snack'?"

"Oh yes!" She nodded violently. "One little bit to fill the mouth, to keep the stomach quiet until later. I know. I will bring souvlakia."

"Not until you tell me what it is, you won't!"

"It is very good!" she assured him. "It is the lumps of lamb-meat on a stick and roasted in the fire."

"Shish kebab without the flames." He shook his head. "Not for me."

"No? Perhaps you like dolmadakia better?"

"What's that, before I get it?"

"It is lamb-meat again, but this time it is minced up very small and with rice, plenty of spices, very good, and wrapped up in grape-leaves. Very delicious!"

"I'd hate to sit down to a real meal, in your terms. No, darling, not that. Look, perhaps just a mouthful or two of soup?"

"Ah! Soupa avgolemonov! I bring!" And before he could halt her she went away, to return rapidly with a generous helping of liquid that his palate deduced was chicken soup flavored with lemon. He consumed it to be sociable, and she made up for this by bringing him a tall glass of orange juice that really was delicious. With the ice thus thoroughly broken, he was able to lead her into casual conversation and prod her, very carefully, into talking about the Argyr Palace and its odd tenant. As far as her language would stand the strain he was able to learn that the countess was locally admired and respected but little known. All anyone ever saw of her was the big black car in which she drove to and from the airport, going or coming back. For the rest she kept to herself, as befitted a lady of title and a widow.

"How about staff? Does she use any local people?"

"Not at all. It is believed that her workpeople come by sea, and go the same way, when she goes away, out of the season, but we never see any of them. She is very private. There is one . . ."

"Yes?"

"A young lady, very beautiful, with blue eyes and yellow hair, very agreeable. Often she comes here, to get food from the market. She is—what do you say?—cook? I have seen her, not spoken. Others say she is friendly but very keen with money, makes a good bargain. Some say she is in charge, is manager-housekeeper and companion. She does not talk much."

Solo kept the voluble waitress a little longer but there was no more to be had from her. In a while he detached himself and strolled away, heading out of the town. According to his map and information the palace was no more than five or six miles away, and he fancied the walk. The exercise gave him time to review the possibilities.

The young blue-eyed blonde cook-housekeeper sounded like his best bet for a contact. Without consciously working it out he had decided that his best play was a frontal attack: he would barge in like the brash tourist he was pretending to be, and trust to his wide-eyed stare to get him through. He was so preoccupied that he completely missed the spread beauty of the scene. Great oaks, walnuts and acacia gave him their shade. In the hedges on either side bloomed hyacinth and honeysuckle, bee-orchis and buttercup. He saw nothing. He was engrossed in other things.

His mind was so busy that his eyes almost missed the sudden and small side road that went precipitously down to his left. This had to lead him close to the Argyr, by his calculations. Five minutes of following it got him within sight of the sea. He halted between high rocky banks and considered his position, then he tackled the rugged wall on his right, scrambling and struggling his way up through the clutching thorns of wild roses, moving through bright splashes of color from wild anemone. Twenty perspiring minutes later he had his reward. He saw the palace, recognizing it at once from the picture he had seen at U.N.C.L.E. head-quarters.

It lay back and away to his right, huddling against the mountain, framed in a fold of rock and backed with the dark green of olive groves. Seen this close it was more Disney-like than ever. The white stone was bright enough to have been freshly laundered and the woodwork of window-frames and shutters was the unlikely pink of cotton candy. A powder-puff palace for a cosmetic surgeon. Resting here on the rock spur he could see something else, too. The main road went by up there. The little side road he had just quitted went straight on down to the sea, to a derelict landing stage. And this rock-spur went straight on down, too, right into the water. So how the devil did you get into the palace grounds?

He clambered higher and over the spur until he could see down the far side, and the riddle was solved. The palace had an extensive forecourt, with an ornamental garden and a drive that led down to a small plage, a place of tiles and seats and a limpid pool. But the private road led on, swung to the left and seemed to plunge headlong into the rockwall. So there had to be a gate, a way through and out into the road. That much was obvious, and he would have come to the gate had he gone on about ten minutes longer down the road. The implications were disturbing. This place was a fort! Only one way in, if you discounted the sea. And that meant there was also only one way out. A good agent, no matter how valiant, likes to know the way out if he has to run.

Solo looked again at the palace, and sighed. Hitching around his "camera" he rested it on a rock and ran out the telescopic lens. If this was Thrush it looked less like it than any place he had ever seen. It was like the concretization of somebody's fairy-tale whim. Still it had to be studied and he proceeded to do that. His acquaintance with architectural styles was meager but he knew enough to guess that this edifice was not of any particular style or period but the work of many hands and various whims. Getting a pinpoint focus he began raking the front, floor by floor. Spires, battlements, and then balconies—and not a sign of life anywhere. The light was against him, so that he couldn't have seen into any of the rooms had he wanted to. But all at once he caught a brief flash of movement and trained his lens back to one of the upper balconies.

There! Something moved, sharpened under his gentle fingers into a slim arm, a hand that moved and clutched something white and fluttering. A sheet, or a towel. In the next moment someone stood up and stretched in a luxurious yawn. He fingered the zoom wheel and the picture ballooned rapidly. A woman, turning now to look down and kick something away clear. She turned again and set her hands on the balcony edge.

Solo held his breath. He was no *voyeur* by choice, but this was a picture to be filed in memory for the sake of it. This was Countess Louise herself as few men could have seen her. Off-guard, unaware of observation and totally unclad, she was like some ancient Greek goddess come alive. Midnight-blue hair caught the sun and shone in a halo around her face. The same sun caressed the magnificent swells and curves of her shape, a shape that any model would have traded her soul to own.

A cynical voice at the back of Solo's mind told him that this woman was a cosmetic surgeon, that the curves were probably artifice, but the part of him that looked through his eyes denied it. This was artless perfection, and innocence. Caution tried to remind him that she was deadly dangerous, but caution was wasting its time. His hand slipped and he swore as he gently nursed the lenses back into line. He saw that she had moved a step or two, to stand by a curious dark object on the balcony wall. Just in time he realized what it was and ducked, turning away and sliding his camera around so that it was out of her sight. A telescope! He should have guessed she would have such a thing. Feeling her eyes on him he swung his head and went through the motions of staring at the scenery. In a while he risked a look in that direction again, and she had vanished out of sight.

He sat and pondered, hard. In the course of a highly exciting life he had learned the virtue of knowing when to run, but he had never learned to like doing it; nor did he now. This place was dangerous. That woman was dangerous. She had just caught him snooping. So his best bet was to depart from there, speedily. But he argued with himself.

"So I run!" he muttered. "Then what? On an island this size, where is there to go?" Having spiked that argument he went on to justify himself. He was playing the part of an irreverent and hard-necked tourist, wasn't he? All right, then, so he was snooping. What could be more natural? Why not carry it through? After all, nobody had taken a shot at him—not yet!

He sat still and surveyed the domain he had come to see. His gaze traveled down the front of the building, to the forecourt and grounds, along the path to the plage, and then on to the sea-front itself. This was almost directly below him. Here someone had built two pier-arms of stone faced with marble out into the sea so that they almost enclosed an area of about an acre of the lazuli-blue water, making it a natural pool. Or a harbor? There was a stone stairway rising out of the water that would be ideal for disembarking from a small boat. Then his eyes found something else.

One of the walls had been built onto the rock-spur where he sat; close to that wall, floating but tethered, was an air-bed. On the air-bed was stretched a slim shape. Another woman. He didn't need his telescope this time to confirm that he was regarding a delectable picture as different from the first as it was possible to get. Blonde—so it had to be the cook-housekeeper.

He secured the camera into its disguised form and set away to scramble down the side of the rock until he could stand on the wall and walk along it. The nearer he got the more he was convinced that he had never in all his life seen a cook who looked like this one. The two scraps of pastel-blue fabric that stood between her and Eve would hardly have made him a handkerchief. The areas thus revealed were golden brown, with all the exuberant loveliness of youth. *No more than twenty-five*, he estimated. *Which is kind of young to be a chef; but she could come and cook for me, any time!*

By the time he stopped walking he could have reached out and touched her. But he didn't. Instead, he used a moment to get back his breath and dignity, then, putting on his best nasal tones, he said:

"Hi, there!"

She snapped awake so suddenly that the air-bed teetered dangerously and it looked as if her bikini was going to get wet. Her eyes *were* blue, and widely indignant as she glared at him.

"Who are you? How did you get here? What do you want?"

"Whoa, now!" He grinned. "One at a time. Matter of fact, I was looking for a castle. I thought I'd found it, but now I'm not so sure."

She stared again, breathing hard. "A castle? What do you mean, you were looking for a castle? Have you lost one?" As he listened, he guessed that she would have a nice voice in more favorable circumstances. By the sound, she came from somewhere very close to the Mason-Dixon line. He poured on the wide-eyed charm.

"That's neat. Have I lost one, hah! Do I look like I would lose a castle, supposing I had one to lose?"

"You look as if you could lose just about anything, including your way. I don't see any road stretching away in back of you. Is it your habit to stroll casually over mountains and into private property?"

"Private?" he queried, and she extended her long arm to point. He looked and saw what he had guessed, a pair of heavy iron gates barring a tunnel cut through the rock.

"Private!" she repeated, and he shrugged.

"I didn't see those. I could see the road going straight on down to the sea, and no castle. I knew it had to be hereabouts someplace. But I don't get it. There isn't a thing in the guide-book about the Achilleion being privately owned. Since when?"

CHAPTER THREE

Now HER blue gaze grew so sharp that he could have
used it for shaving. "You," she said, "are either a stupid
fool, or a terrible liar. Which is it, Mr. . . . ?"

"Summers. Nathan Summers. You don't leave me a
great deal of choice there, Miss . . . ?"

"My name is Winter. Katherine Winter."

He grinned. This was an unexpected bonus and he
grasped it quickly. "That's one for the book, isn't it?
Summers—Winter! What d'you know! And what a chilly
name for a pretty—er—warm-looking kind of person.
Doesn't suit you at all."

She thawed a little, but not much. "You still haven't
answered my question, Mr. Summers. Let me put
you into the picture just a little. In the first place, this is
not a castle. The only castle I know of, in this region,
is in town. This is a palace. There is a difference. In
the second place, this is *not* the Achilleion. Frankly, I
do not see how anybody could possibly make such a
mistake as that, especially someone with a guide-book.
And in the third and most important place, this is private property, and it says so, clearly, on the other side
of those gates. Now, Mr. Summers?"

"Three strikes and out," he admitted cheerfully.,
"You certainly make me sound like a Grade A cluck. But
look at it from where I am. In the book it says the
Achilleion is about seven or eight miles south of town.

31

So I walk. It's a nice day and I like walking. But after a while I begin to wonder. I know you don't expect to see signposts stuck up in the middle of the road saying 'This way to the Achilleion,' nor would you look for a palace—or a castle—right there *beside* the road. But there has to be some signs of life! And I had walked just a bit more than I bargained for. So I suspected it was tucked away someplace. Then I saw a side road. So I wandered a little. And I was right. It certainly is tidily tucked away! But now you tell me this isn't the Achilleion at all! Now what kind of a deal is it when somebody owns a palace, private?"

"This is the Argyr Palace," she told him, very firmly. "It is the private residence of the Countess de St-Denis."

"Oh, sure!" he nodded in heavy irony. "You're a beautiful princess and she's the wicked stepmother, and I'm a knight in shining armor, only it's all enchanted and doesn't show until I kiss you and break the spell. Where have I heard that story before? And you're not doing it right, you know. You're supposed to be shut up in a tower, on bread and water. Come off it, sister. The Countess de San-whatsit—that's French. I don't want to be thought bright, but I do know that much. And this is Greece. What are you trying to hand me, hey?" He turned to look at the cotton candy palace and then came back to her again. "Or are you trying to cover up? What is it, a laughing-academy for the better-class dim-domes?"

"A what?" she demanded, completely baffled.

"You know, the kind of place you put rich Uncle George in when he starts thinking he's a turkey and laying eggs all over the place. You know, a rest-home?"

"Mr. Summers!" She was scandalized. "Do I look like a wardress in a lunatic asylum?"

"No. Not even an inmate," he told her enthusiastically. "I don't know you well enough to tell you just how you look, to me. But what you do not look like, one hundred percent for sure, is French aristocracy. Nor do you sound like it. For that matter, you're no Corfiote, either. You're as American as I am. Your turn!"

"I have never tried to suggest that I am anything but American—not that it is any of your business. I work here. I manage the domestic side of her ladyship's affairs. If you must know, I'm a cook-housekeeper. And I have no intention whatever of losing my job through indiscretions with you. May I remind you, for the last time, this is private property. I think I had better escort you to the gate and out." She reached for the mooring-rope, hauled the air-bed in close, and accepted his helping hand to step up and out onto the wall. This close, she smelled like some new kind of perfume. Solo allowed his expression to dissolve into chagrin.

"I do believe you're not kidding. Are you? This is for real, the countess and everything?"

"Of course!" She stepped past him and began to lead the way, very decoratively, to the path.

"Look," he pleaded, following her, "I didn't do any harm. All right, so I'm a fool, but maybe I could meet the countess and explain . . . ?"

"I hardly think so. Madame sees very few guests, and those only by special arrangements. Her desire for privacy is quite genuine."

"Squashed again. Miss Winter, I have to apologize to somebody, just to prove that I have nice manners. How about you? You can't cook-housekeep all the time. When's

33

your night out?" They came to the tiled stretch, and she stopped to gather a pair of rope-soled slippers, then, as she came erect again, she sighed.

"I'm sorry, Mr. Summers. I had hoped to avoid this, but I'm afraid you really are in trouble this time!"

Following the direction of her gaze, he saw a curious little vehicle coming rapidly toward them from the palace, along the gray-black roadway. It was silent, rubber-tired, with a double-seat in front and a locker-box behind, looking something like a golf-cart. One glance sufficed for the vehicle. The occupant deserved more, and got it from him. Solo studied her openly as the cart purred right up to them and stopped. The beauty that had warmed his eyes at a distance lost nothing at all by being seen close at hand. If anything, it was enhanced, and, for once in his long and adventurous career, Solo found himself face to face with a woman who defied all his attempts at analysis.

He could, and did, catalogue the details. Her hair was so black as to be blue where the sun caught it, and her eyes were so dark as to be almost the same color. Her complexion was the hue of fine honey. Her shape, a combination of bountiful curves and willowy slenderness, stopped just a breath short of exaggeration, and should have seemed outrageous, but didn't. And that was where the magic started. He had seen all these bits and pieces before, on other women, and they were in no way unique, nor was her wisp-of-white bikini a new experience to him. But there was something in the way all these thing went together that made this woman considerably more than just the sum total of all the parts.

There was a glow, he thought, that wasn't just on

the surface but came from some power-source deep down inside her. And, though she stood quite still once she had dismounted from the cart, he had the sensation of seething motion, in the same way that a spinning flywheel only *looks* as if it is standing still. Insanely, he felt sure that if he touched her he would feel a shock! Then, becoming aware that he was staring at her, he drew a trembling breath and manufactured a smile. The lady looked right through him, then turned her head.

"Kate, who is this man and what is he doing here?"

Her voice matched her looks and set the seal on the whole of her. It was a full round contralto, like a cellostring bowed by a master hand. Solo expressed a shiver, remembering the warning, "This woman is dangerous!"

"I'm sorry, Madame, I really don't know. He *says* he was looking for the Achilleion, and was under the impression that he had found it."

The dark eyes swiveled back to Solo, and now they really had fires in them. Scorn infused her lovely face.

"The Achilleion? Bah!" Emphasis agitated her curves alarmingly. "You must be a simpleton, *monsieur*, or a fool, to mistake my palace for that dreary museum of relics. Kindly regard it!" She flung a hand, a slim arm, to point. "Does it look like an ancient Greek monument?"

Solo struggled for composure. This was the contact he had hoped for but never really expected to make so soon or so easily, and now, just when he needed all his wits, they were tangled.

"Your palace?" he queried unsteadily.

Miss Winter came to his rescue. "Mr. Nathan Summers, you are speaking to the Countess Anne-Marie Louise de St-Denis!"

Solo had no need to pretend his distress. He could

feel the sweat standing out on his face. Hoping that his dazed expression would pass for typical title-worshiping humility, he mumbled:

"Gosh! A countess! A real live French countess!"

The vision smiled suddenly, and it was as if someone had put a match to a torch—and cast light into a dark place. It was a vivid and beautiful smile. He struggled to make words.

"You'll have to excuse me, your ladyship. Gosh, I'm honored, real honored!" He offered his hand. It was ignored utterly. He looked at it and let it fall again. The countess laughed, and all at once his mind was full of parallels. Just like this Poppaea might have laughed at the first announcement of Christians-to-the-lions week. Or Helen of Troy at the big launching. Or Salome . . . Solo brought his imagination back from the images and tried to be calm.

"You are surprised, Mr. Summers?" she challenged. "First you cannot tell the difference between an old castle and my own beautiful palace, and now you are confused because I am a countess and I look just like any other woman. Are you always so *derange* as this?" It was open mockery, and just what was needed to snap his wits into their more normal efficiency. His smile came easier now.

"It's just not my day, I reckon. But honest, how could I know it was the wrong place until I'd seen it? Soon as I did, I suspected it was wrong. As I told Miss Winter here, it's not a bit the way I heard."

"It is perhaps not so good?"

"Ah, now, I didn't say that. How can I tell? I haven't seen the other place yet. I'll say this: if it's better than this it sure must be some place!"

"Mine is better," she told him flatly. "You understand such things?"

"I'm no expert, but I do have an eye for beauty, of any kind. And I hate to contradict anyone, but you don't look just like any other woman."

"You think I am beautiful, yes?" She threw out the challenge openly, but he grinned and took it, appreciating that she was trying to keep him in the wrong. The candid type. He could be candid, too.

"Put it this way," he said, frankly. "I don't know all that many titled ladies, not to be familiar with, but I think you'd beat them all. In a way, it's a crime . . ."

"What is a crime?" she demanded quickly, as he paused.

"Oh, nothing. Just the way you're hid out here. On a remote little island, and tucked away in this palace, and, so Miss Winter says, you have very few guests. That's all wrong. What I mean, if I hadn't stumbled on this place by accident I would never have seen you. And just think what I would have missed!"

It was a critical moment. Had he piled it on a bit too thick? This woman was no fool. Had she seen through him? After a pause, her smile gave him the answer. He could have used it for any welding job.

"So *gauche*," she said. "But so sweet, too. I like you. And yes, sometimes I have guests. You will come to dinner this evening."

"Ah, now!" He put up a protesting hand. "I wasn't fishing . . ."

"Zut! Say no more. It arranged itself, and it pleases me. A Frenchman would have used twice as many words and meant less. You will come. I will send the car for you. Where?"

"I'm at the Palace," he told her, then laughed. "I mean the Palace Hotel, of course. You're very kind. Formal?"

"*Quoi?*" She was momentarily baffled, then nodded. "You mean, shall you dress up in a stiff shirt? But now you look comfortable. Why change? I shall be the one to dress up. You shall see!" She wheeled away from him without a further word, moved to the back of her vehicle and lifted a lid to pull out a bundle of fleecy white towels which she dropped on the tiles. Turning back to him, she put out her hand.

"Now I shall swim a little before *dejeuner*. And I shall look forward to this evening. *Au 'voir*, Mr. Summers.

It seemed only natural to take her hand and raise it to his lips, so he did that. She seemed pleased.

"*Alors*, Kate!" she said. "You will take the cart and give Mr. Summers a ride up the hill as far as the main road, yes? It is not right he should walk so far on such a hot day!"

It wasn't all the heat of the day, he thought wryly. Solo realized he was perspiring freely as he settled beside Miss Winter in the double front-seat of the cart. Using his handkerchief, he said:

"She's quite a girl. Was that me, or is she always like that?"

"She's impulsive, but I never knew her to invite a perfect stranger to visit, like that. Just what is your game, Mr. Summers?"

"Whoa now!" he sighed. "Don't let's start that again. I already told you . . ."

"You've tried to tell me that you are just a casual tourist looking for the Achilleion and that you found the Argyr Palace by accident."

"And?"

"I don't believe you. For just one thing, you're carrying a camera, but you didn't attempt to take any pictures!"

"So what do *you* think I am?" Solo offered her the chance to talk, wondering what was in her mind. In his own was the strange awareness that this girl was every bit as lovely as the countess and yet totally different in her presence. She exuded a pleasantly warm glow, whereas the other one tended to make a man boil. Odd stuff, chemistry!

"I think you're a fortune-hunter," she said, quite positively. "Her ladyship is extremely wealthy, very beautiful, and a widow."

"And what are you?" he wondered aloud. "Part-time guard dog?"

"That's uncalled for!" she snapped. "But, if you must know, I'm safeguarding my own interests. I have a very good position here, and I intend to keep it. So, I ask you again, just what are you after?"

The trundling cart came now to the large steel gates. Miss Winter got down to operate a push-button that sent them sighing wide open, then she rejoined him and the cart purred out into the road, making a left-hand turn uphill.

"Seriously," he murmured, "I've done a lot of things in my time, but marrying a woman for her money has never been one of them. You said she was a widow?"

"Four times!" she said, with just a tinge of malice.

"There you are! I'm not about to become the fifth, at anything. But, and I wouldn't kid you, I am curious. You say she has money. How? Did she marry it?"

"Not all of it, no. She owns the St-Denis laboratories, in Paris. And she's a world-famous cosmetic surgeon!"

"Hah!" he said, pretending surprise and enlightenment. "That's where I've heard the name before. Cosmetic surgeon? So that's where she gets the Cleopatra shape from."

"Don't be ridiculous!" Miss Winter retorted sharply. "That shape is her own. At least . . ."

"The whole point about cosmetic surgery," he pointed out, "is that you can't tell the difference. For all I know, you may be one of her best customers, or a sample product."

"How would you like to get off and walk?" she invited icily, and he stifled a grin at the fury in her voice.

"No offense intended, honest. Only making the point that if it is expertly done you can't tell the difference. All the same, though, I don't see how she could do surgery on herself, so I take it all back. Anyway, you're just the cook-housekeeper, nothing else, eh?"

"Absolutely nothing else. I have no connection with her business and I mind my own. I would advise you to do the same, Mr. Summers."

"Call me Nathan," he invited. "I have the feeling you don't trust me, Kate. I wish there was something I could do to convince you that I'm on the level."

She halted the cart with the main road just in front of them and turned to him, a curious expression on her face. Then she got down and waited for him to follow, so that she could point.

"You can't go wrong from here. It's that way. Mr. Summers. . . . Nathan, there's something I can do, if you'll promise me you won't get any wrong impressions. It's the only way I know for telling a good man from a bad one. May I?"

"Go ahead." He eyed her warily. All at once she

surged close and threw her long arms around his neck, capturing his mouth with hers. By the time she released him they were both breathing considerably faster.

"Did I pass the test?" he demanded, and she sighed.

"I think so. I'm not absolutely sure, but whatever you are up to, it can't be all that bad!" With that she spun around and climbed back into the cart, sending it purring away back down the little road, leaving him standing with a frown.

After a while, he started back for the hotel, walking slowly and struggling to shuffle his ideas into some kind of rational pattern, but he hadn't quite succeeded even by the time he had reached his hotel and was sitting on his bed. He had one thing in common with Katherine Winter. He wasn't quite sure what she was up to, but he *was* sure it wasn't all bad. And yet she was up to *something*. Whoever heard of a Frenchwoman with an American cook?

For the rest of his mental ingredients he had less assurance. He stirred them and shook his head at the suspicious flavor that came off. He had confirmed, definitely, that Countess Louise was highly dangerous, but not in the way he had been led to expect. With her looks and that built-in volcanic appeal she could have charmed birds off a tree, but that she was crooked, or evil, in the Thrush sense of the word, he found hard to believe. And yet, he reminded himself, there was Stanton. She had got him, somehow. Or had she? Perhaps her function had been no more than as bait for a trap? In which case he needed to think hard about the unexpected invitation to dinner. He was still thinking it over as he used his radio to get in touch with Waverly. Number One, Section One, was not pleased to hear the account.

"You have disobeyed my cautions, Mr. Solo. I went to a great deal of trouble to warn you that the woman was dangerous, yet you've walked right into her coils."

"Hardly that, sir. I'm reporting from my hotel room. I'm not 'caught' in any way. And look what I've got. The lady has taken a fancy to me, invited me into her home."

"Walk into my parlor!"

"That's possible, of course, but I can't see why. She doesn't know who I am. In any case, if it is a trap of some kind—well—vainly is the net spread in the sight of the bird. I'm not going into this with my eyes shut, after all!"

Waverly snorted irritably. "Mr. Solo, I am aware that your attitude toward a pretty woman is that of an angler toward trout in a stream, but one of these days you are going to hook a shark. And this could be the day. I'm aware that you're forewarned, and that you are resourceful, but you should bear in mind that thin ice is not dangerous except to those who insist upon skating on it. I strongly suggest you consider evading that invitation to dinner."

"I'll see what turns up, sir," Solo said, and put his instrument away with a wry grin. It was indicative of Waverly's state of mind that he "suggested" rather than "ordered." It was a difficult situation. Solo recalled the countess and her dazzling smile, and felt a tiny chill. But somebody had to take a chance . . . and when would there be a better time?

CHAPTER FOUR

DR. SUSAN HARVEY, making a bid to deal with growing frustration, took up the glass cover of a petri dish and began, quite unnecessarily, to polish it with a tissue. Tilted at the correct angle, and with the dark gloss of the laboratory bench to back it, the glass made a good mirror. She studied her reflection carefully. Objectively, putting aside silly modesty, she knew she was attractive. Her pale blonde hair, cut short and shaped to her head, gleamed silkily. She had on the minimum of effective makeup, all she needed. She had a shape, too, although the laboratory smock didn't do much for it. Still, she thought irritably, I'm not a hag! So why?

She shifted her gaze to stare offendedly at the sober-faced straw-haired young man who sat opposite her at the bench. Why? For all the effect she was having on him she might well have been just part of the equipment! Didn't he ever relax and become human? As if stirred by her thought, he chose that moment to look up from the volume he was studying, and met her gaze with eyes as blue as her own, staring at her impersonally. Instantly she felt foolish and confused, and as hot as if she had just been dropped into a warm bath. His words came blurrily over the roar of blood in her ears.

"Is this all the reference you have, Dr. Harvey, on electrical stimulation of the cortex?"

"That?" She struggled to order her wits. "Oh! Yes. I can get more if you really want to go into it. But that's hardly a field for bio-chemistry research, which is what you're supposed to be studying."

"Yes, I know." He sounded apologetic. "This book deals mostly with the immune reaction to artificial implants in the body. I suppose that's why you have it in your library here."

"Immunology *is* my special field," she reminded him, perhaps a shade more tartly than she intended, and he nodded.

"I know. I'm very grateful to you for taking the time to tutor me in the general background. There's such a lot of it nowadays. If I was going into it for real I would go for medical electronics, I think."

"You'd still have to cover the basic field of bio-chemistry before specializing. Everyone has to do that."

He seemed to become aware that she was not in the best of moods, and stirred uneasily. "Look. Dr. Harvey, I'm sorry to be taking up such a lot of your time. It must be tedious for you."

Self-control withered in her mind. She took a deep breath. "Now look!" she declared, laying her hands flat on the bench. "Kindly stop apologizing. Stop thinking you are wasting my time. Section One asked me to take you on a quick tour of bio-chemistry, and I am trying to do that. Glad to do it. And you are a good pupil, too. But . . ."

"But what?"

"But we have been at this now for almost three days and you are still calling me Dr. Harvey, for heaven's sake! Your name's Illya and mine's Susan. Will it hurt if we are friends?"

His eyes were still cool and impersonal as he looked at her. "You've never dealt directly with a field agent before, have you, Doc—I mean—Susan?"

"No," she said, and then repeated it: "No."

"Just for the record," he smiled faintly—"I *am* human. And it can be a nuisance, sometimes. Like now. At the outside I have two more days to spare, a lot to learn, and no leeway for making mistakes."

"I appreciate that, of course. I would hate to have anything put me off *my* work. But I'm human too. One doesn't have to be so dedicated all the time, surely. It can't hurt to take just five minutes off for the social amenities?"

"Five seconds can be fatal, at the wrong time. In this job you're either dedicated, or dead. You have just one idea in mind, and no time for anything else. That can be difficult, too. Right now I have the feeling there's an idea trying to push into my mind and upset things."

"You've made your point!" she snapped. "There's no need to push it."

"I didn't mean you. Something to do with this." He took up the book again, still open at the page he had been studying. "Something about the auto-immune reaction in the brain area and metal tolerance . . ."

"The brain chemistry differs. Its whole circulation is different. That's what we call the blood-brain barrier. Just as well. The body can be poisoned and the brain remain normal in many cases, and there are only a few chemicals which affect the brain directly . . ."

She was interrupted by the telephone. Picking it up, she listened, then offered it to him. "For you. From the radio-research room."

"Thank you." Kuryakin took it. "Mike?"

"Right. I think we have something, Illya. Those modules are silver-plated. Makes for better skin-contact, I suppose, and they need body-heat to operate. Anyway, that silver sheath causes a resonance-field that we can detect. I can fix you a little monitor that will tell you whenever you're within—say—fifty feet of one of them in action. Handy?"

"Very much so. Nice work. Let me know when you have it going." Kuryakin put down the receiver and sat quite still, so much so that Susan Harvey frowned at him.

"Now what?"

"Probably nothing." He shivered and then smiled. "Just a word. Silver wires into the brain. Silver-plating on those modules. Forget it. Now, about the breakdown products of adrenalin . . ."

Napoleon Solo dressed himself slowly and with care, including about his person every weapon of offense and defense he could contrive without being too spectacular. Although he would never have admitted as much to Waverly or anyone else, he had a rooted dislike for entering a trap without due care, and was under no illusion at all as to how dangerous the Argyr Palace could be. His only card, that the countess could have no idea of his real identity, was a slender one, but he had no intention of backing out and thus discarding his whole hand. In good time he wandered down to the bar for a quick bracer, but never got that far. As he crossed the bright-lit foyer a vision in blue satin appeared, making him halt and breathe deeply in appreciation.

"For me?" he inquired, going over to her. "I'm honored that the countess should have sent you in person. But who's cooking dinner?"

"I have it in control," she told him tartly. "If you're quick, we can get back before it's cooked to death. She won't allow anybody but herself, or me, to touch her shiny new Mercedes."

"I wouldn't expect her to come herself, naturally. All right . . ."

"You have about five minutes to pack."

"Pack?"

"That's right, pack. You're to stay at the palace. Well?" Her tone had edges now. "What are you waiting for? Don't you want to come and stay?"

The negative trembled on his tongue but he swallowed it simply because he couldn't think of a plausible reason to refuse. Five minutes later, with his bag tossed in the back and himself seated beside her as she drove, he still couldn't think of anything except the obvious question.

"Why this sudden effusion of hospitality on the part of the countess? What did I do?"

"As if you didn't know!" she retorted. "You're the Casanova type. For those who like that kind of thing, that is."

"But not you," he said, grinning. "I think you flatter me just a bit. I can't see somebody like the countess losing any sleep over me. I'd guess it's much more likely that she expects to have a bit of sport at my expense."

"And you don't mind?"

"Not a bit. I can take a joke. You could help if you can tell me whether she has arranged anything special for my—er—entertainment?"

He kept his tone light, but there was a serious purpose

under his words and he listened carefully for her reaction. It was slow to come. A side-glance showed him that she was scowling ahead at the road as if in thought.

"You know," she murmured, "you could be right. Just after lunch she told me there was to be company tonight. Four distinguished guests. Of course I asked if there was any special kind of dish she had in mind, and I mentioned you by name, saying that you were American, and would be no trouble. Her guests, as a rule, are foreign, you see. But when I mentioned you, she laughed. 'Mr. Summers,' she said, 'is hardly a guest. I doubt if I could sell *him* anything. But we must feed him, of course. So you must count five, not four.' And then, later, when I asked if she wanted me to take the car and pick you up, she added the bit about packing your bag. You can make what you like out of that."

He made quite a lot of it and liked none of it, but knew that it was much too late to turn back now. As his mind raced to compute the possible permutations of peril be asked: "Sell? What would she be trying to sell me?"

"Oh!" Miss Winter laughed cynically. "You'll see. I've heard her a few times. She has a thing about being beautiful. Thinks it's everyone's duty to be as attractive as possible. It can get quite embarrassing at times, the way she will pick out somebody's faults and analyze them, and then go on to explain how easy it would be to correct them. Surgery, of course."

"Not there and then, in the palace, surely?"

"I don't think so. I believe she could, though. She has some very elaborate equipment on the spot. *I* haven't seen it. But I do know she gets things, chemicals and stuff, and gadgetry. I'm always picking up packages for her, whenever I come into town for groceries."

"She keeps you pretty busy," he said, speaking automatically while he stared at the horrid fact that he was being transported straight into a Thrush gathering. "Four distinguished guests" could hardly be anything else; and if any one of them recognized him, his fat was in for a burning time. "Cook, housekeeper, chauffeur, and you do your own grocery shopping. Doesn't she have any other staff?"

"Oh yes." Miss Winter's tone was definitely cool now. "She has a local man in from time to time to do the grounds and so on. And there's Adam, of course."

"Who's he?"

"You'll see." There was a chill silence for a while, then she said, reverting to her former theme: "Just don't laugh when she starts on about the body beautiful. She takes that kind of thing very seriously."

Despite the desperate situation, Solo had to grin. "I can't wait to see her sales pitch. I'll bet it's something terrific, with the assets she has. She might even sell me on a nose retread."

Miss Winter sniffed. "I'd always thought French women were—well—subtle. You know? But she is downright crude at times. She doesn't hint at all. She comes right out with it."

"I had noticed."

"You know, she once said to me, 'Marie Antoinette achieved her fame because she was a beautiful woman and was not ashamed of it. She had a bigger bust than Jayne Mansfield. And mine is bigger still!' Imagine anyone bothering to point out a thing like that. As if it mattered!"

Solo grinned again, but without much mirth. The picture he saw for himself was bleak in the extreme. She halted the car for the gate, got out and inserted her long arm through the bars to operate the button, and then they drove in and up to the courtyard of the palace, under a low-pitched archway that faced a short flight of marble steps up to the main door. As they climbed the steps, yellow light spilled out into the dusk from the open doors. Once inside, a mosaic floor repeated his footsteps loudly. The distant walls on either side were painted and pillared, the pillars set at intervals of one yard. Between each pillar was a pedestal, and each pedestal was occupied by a white stone statue. Solo tried to take it all in with one comprehensive glance but then he had to halt and look again. He lifted his brows.

"You'll get used to it," Miss Winter told him. "They shook me at first, but after a while you have to admit they are extremely good."

She was quite right. He cast his eye again over the array of nudes, and nodded. Seen all at once, they were overpowering, but when he devoted time to studying each one, he had to admit that the sculptor had created something very close to perfection. The idealized human form in either sex and in many different attitudes could hardly be bettered as inspiration for someone so fanatically devoted to making people beautiful. And there she was herself, standing in the far doorway, awaiting him.

Solo strode boldly forward with a smile. For the occasion, she had put on a billowing froth of white stuff that began low on her bosom and drifted to the floor in delicate folds. As she moved toward him the garment swirled like white mist. She gave him her hand, with a dazzling smile.

"You are welcome, Mr. Summers. How do you like my figures? Do you think they have better ones in the Achilleion?"

"I doubt," he said, "that anyone can improve on perfection. Miss Winter tells me your work is to improve the appearance, but if this is the standard you're aiming at you must be pretty frustrated. Ordinary humans can't hope to look like that."

"Perhaps not. They are ideal. I had them specially made for me. I have others, as you shall see. But now you must come and meet my guests."

She led him through the door into a room that would have made him breathless by itself, but he had very little time to waste on it. One fast glance was all he could spare for the precious carpet on the floor, the magnificent tapestries that clothed the walls, the carved and brocaded furnishings, and the glowingly painted ceiling. In the next breath he was staring at the company and realizing his worst fears.

"Señor Salvador Morales," she said. "Mr. Summers." And Solo met the dark eyes of the gray-haired and leonine old conquistador, watching for a glimmer of recognition. But none came, to his relief, for Solo knew *him* well enough as the controlling brain behind Thrush-Madrid. He bowed, moved on, and confronted a thickset, almost bald man with a bristle moustache and glass-cold gray eyes. The countess told him, although he hardly needed telling, that this was "Herr Doktor Heinrich Klasser." Solo knew his nickname as "Killer Klasser," and that he had his own unspeakable ways

51

with experimental surgery, on subjects who were never asked to volunteer.

Next was a hulking, black-browed, black-haired bull of a man whom she introduced as Ricco Vassi, known to Solo as covering vast areas of Italy, his job being to superintend and expedite any operations commanded by his Thrush seniors. Fourth and last was a lean and patrician elder, who rested one gracious elbow on a carved mantlepiece and wore his dignity like a cloak. When his hostess called this man Dr. Andre Cabari, of Uruguay, Solo had to think hard for a moment. Then he had it. Social scientist, crowd manipulator, revolutionary, the man who made things happen in quiet but devastating ways, merely by talking carefully to the right people at the right time.

What a bunch! Solo carefully drew a deep breath and realized he was perspiring. He used his handkerchief.

"It's a warm night," he pointed out, and the countess shook a finger at him in criticism.

"You are out of condition. You Americans! All the time you worry about plumbing, but you never seem to realize that there are other ways of keeping the body clean. You neglect the largest organ of the body."

Before he could protest, the sound of a brazen gong shivered on the air and a pair of massive double-doors swung back. She took his arm and led him into a dining room that would have put Hollywood's most lavish movie set to shame. The marble floor gleamed. A long refectory table stood in the middle of a priceless carpet. Tapestries and shawls glowed on the walls and a fountain chattered happily to itself within a recess that might once have been a stately fireplace but was now an indoor garden. Light from four glorious chandeliers reflected the gleaming polished wood of the table and the glittering glass and silver which were arranged on it.

But what caught Solo's eye and held it for a breathless second was yet another member of the gathering. This man stood erect like a footman just inside the door and at first glance would have passed for another of the statues, except that he was flesh-colored. It cost Solo a second look and a near-stumble to be sure, then the countess laughed gently in his ear.

"That is Adam, who will wait on us. You still think ordinary humans cannot be perfect?"

He was still trying to think of a good reply as they settled in their seats. These were huge carved chairs that had obviously come from some cathedral, and he would have wondered at them and all the other magnificent pieces that filled the room, if there had not been so much on his mind that he could only dredge up folly.

"There's nothing wrong with my liver, Countess!" he protested, and it took her a moment or two to hark back to their previous gambit. Then she laughed again.

"Your liver? Oh no, Mr. Summers. I meant your skin. It is a doctor's joke, you see. The skin is the largest organ of the body. You did not know that? It is true. And it is much more important than you think. How much of your skin can breathe? Only your face and hands. That is bad. Look, my garment allows all my skin to breathe. You see?" She struck a pose that made her point strikingly obvious, then gestured to the living statue she had called Adam. The six-foot-three herculean figure was now in catlike motion, bringing dishes and a salver. Solo looked. The man wore only a loin-cloth in stark white, and his face was absolutely expressionless. "You see my Adam, also, see how perfect he is?" She spoke quite loudly but the servile giant showed not a sign of having heard. The countess swept the rest of the company with an arrogant eye and proceeded to elaborate.

"The skin is a remarkable thing, the foundation of all true health. For example, it is the only body tissue that is alive on one side and dead on the other. Think of that!" She stretched a forefinger to prod Adam's arm as he leaned over her with a plate. Then she curled the finger around to touch her own bosom. "A dead outer shell, in both cases. The living tissue is on the other side."

Solo began to sweat again. This woman was a nut about health and beauty, just as Miss Winter had warned him. He was so engrossed in trying to keep track of everything, listening, watching the other members of the feast, that he missed the first taste of his soup altogether. The second spoonful tickled his attention and the third insisted on it. He tasted, then turned to Miss Winter, who had taken the vacant seat by his left hand.

"You certainly are a cook. This never came out of a can!"

"Glad you like it." She smiled shyly. "It's really simple, though. Just green pea, but with added sour cream and wine." He savored the soup again, noting that the others also approved. Adam brought the next dish, and Miss Winter looked a little apprehensive. Solo employed knife and fork, bit, chewed and swallowed, then sighed. "What is it? Or them?"

"You approve?"

"I most definitely do. My stomach will think I'm dead at last and in heaven. Why?"

"I call them beef-marrow dumplings. Chopped beef-marrow bulked out with bread-crumbs, spiced with wild thyme and grated lemon rind, bonded with egg and boiled in a strong meat stock. I made quite a lot, if you want more."

He did. So did the others, in various accents. Then came a salad that was crisper and tastier than he would have believed possible, and a layer-cake so delicious that he felt regret at not having room enough for a third helping. By the time Adam brought the wine and the coffee Solo was sure of two things. One, that he was full and happy; two, that Kate Winter was no crook. Cook, yes. Crook, no. Nobody with a criminal mind could possibly come so close to being divine!

Then Miss Winter bade everyone good night and departed, and the table atmosphere modulated suddenly and subtly. Countess Louise lost her beaming charm and seemed to be engrossed in some rapid chatter with the others, each in his own tongue and in argot, which Solo could follow only with a great deal of difficulty. German, French, Italian or Spanish, those he could manage, provided the speaker spoke slowly and was prepared to be patient with him. But he had no chance at all as these five people plunged into a quick-fire torrent of interchange in slang and cant phrases. In a while he took what he thought was the offered hint and created a yawn, stifling it with a palm. The countess had her eyes on him in a flash.

"You are bored, Mr. Summers?"

"Call it tired. I've had a big day. And this air. And the food."

"I see." She eyed him, and there were fires in those eyes. "Would you prefer to retire to your room now?"

"If that's all right with you, yes."

"Very well. We have some business to discuss, but it will not take all night. Come . . ." She rose briskly and led him to the door, summoning the silent Adam with a crook of her finger. Outside, she halted and brought on her dazzling smile. "Business is so boring. Tomorrow will be another day, yes?" Before he could anticipate it, she surged close and put her long arms around his neck, drawing his head down. He would have been less than human if he had not responded in the most natural way. By the time she released him his head was reeling and his breath was coming fast.

"There!" she whispered. "*Dormez bien*. Perhaps the talk will be not too long. Maybe I shall see you again, soon?"

Then she was gone and Adam had his suitcase and was padding impassively on ahead toward a staircase. Solo followed, wondering whether he was on the polished floor or walking in mid-air.

CHAPTER FIVE

It was quite a room. In any other circumstances Solo would have been impressed by it. Now he inspected it simply as a routine precaution, touching the wall hangings, trying the door, then studying his bemused face in the triple mirrors of a magnificent dressing-table by the window. He was not quite conceited enough to believe that Countess Louise was pulling out all the stops on him simply because of his male charm. There had to be a catch somewhere. Something was hatching inside that beautifully decorated skull of hers. But what? He was absolutely certain he was in for trouble, but just as certain that he didn't know what kind. At last he settled on the bed edge and reached for his communicator, feeling relief in being able to call on routine.

Waverly needed to know about the Thrush gathering, if nothing else. He drew out the extension antenna, thumbed the switch and was about to ask for Overseas Relay, when the words halted on his tongue. The instrument in his hand gave off a steady crackling whine of interference. He glared at in in unbelief, switched off, then on again, jarred it with the heel of his hand, but still the smothering crackle persisted. Now the flesh really began to creep on the back of his neck. Either his talker had developed a defect, which was highly unlikely, to say the least, or somebody had rigged this area—this room—with a jammer! And that logical assumption carried with it so many other inferences that he was up off the bed and on his feet before he had added up all of them.

The communicator went away with a practiced move that drew his pistol on the return. He started for the door, then halted as there came a soft tapping. Crouching a little, he called, "Who is it?"

The door swung open and the countess stood there a moment, then came in, her eyes widening at sight of his weapon.

"Why?" she whispered. "You will not need that!"

"Stop right there. I don't trust you any closer than you are right now. Back up and turn around. You and I are taking a little walk."

"So unnecessary," she pouted, then turned obediently, but not to go out of the door again. Instead she caught it, pushed it shut, then set her back to it, facing him. "You have nothing to fear," she said, and smiled. "See, I am unarmed." And she did something rapidly to the rear of her dress, spread her arms wide, and the rustling white material fell to the floor.

She was definitely unarmed, unless one could count the volcanic beauty of her unclad curves. Solo froze for a moment that was his undoing. A large hand swung down and across from his right side, numbing his wrist, to send the pistol skidding across the floor. He ducked and sprang away from the movement, and found himself face to face with Adam.

Over that muscular shoulder he saw a gaping hole where the dressing-table had swung away from the wall. He caught a glimpse of the countess as she swooped nakedly to snatch up his gun. Then, catlike, he went forward to meet the impassive servant. Adam

showed no more expression than a shop window figure, but waited silently, arms down and out, ready.

Solo feinted a left, leaped and chopped down with
all his strength and weight in a right-hand neck-breaker.
Adam, with perfect anticipation, leaned and tensed his
muscles—and the chop bounced, shocking Solo's arm
right up to his elbow. Surging in the opposite direction,
the statuesque servant swung a haymaking righthander,
low down, that contacted Solo's ribs and bombed him
bodily backward, smashing all the wind out of him. If
there was science in this, it was none that Solo had
ever met before.

With that kind of strength, who needed science?

Fighting off the instinct to curl up, wheezing for
breath, he shambled forward again. It was no time for
delicacy. He poised himself, then leaned and launched
a kick where it would do maximum damage. But Adam
had speed out of all reason in a man of his bulk. An
arm like a beam swept down and across, smashed
into Solo's shin as it came up, knocked it aside so
that he spun and almost fell, cringing as his weight
came on that leg. It felt broken. Then Adam moved
in, taking the offensive. Again that bombing right hand
to the body.

Solo reeled away, slammed into the wall, staggered
forward and right into a left fist that came down like
a hammer on the top of his head.

The room grew a big black hole and he fell into it
head first. The countess came to stand and stare down
at the ruin.

"A valiant one. Clever, too. I can use one such." She
turned to her servant, who was not even out of breath,
and smiled, pointing down. "Bring him!" She moved

away to gather up her discarded dress and looped it carelessly over one arm, then she preceded her servant through the secret door and into the passage there. Adam crouched, picked up Solo like a sack, hung him over one shoulder, and followed her, drawing the dressing-table flush to the wall as he went.

In the tower-room at the other end of the passage, Katherine Winter put down her pen, lit a cigarette and leaned back to let her mind have its own way with the vexing problem of Mr. Nathan Summers. She was in the middle of her weekly letter to Uncle Otto, a rambling and inane epistle, mostly gossip and trivia, but which contained full descriptive details of everyone who had visited the Argyr Palace that week. It was her report, and Uncle Otto was no relative at all, but an elderly, ruddy-faced military gentleman who would skip all the banalities, but who would be very careful to list all the personalities and arrange to have them investigated. So she had been told.

The gentleman had approached her immediately after she had secured the job with the countess. He had been very polite and laden with official documents to prove his authority. She believed he was C.I.A. but had not inquired too deeply about this. On his advice, it was better for her to know as little as possible, thus making it impossible for her to give anything away, even by accident. All he wanted, and he was careful to stress this, was the name, nationality and time of arrival and departure of any guests. She was to supply these in the weekly letter. And do nothing more. At all.

From which facts Kate had gathered that she was involved in something very dangerous. She had been unwilling to help, but was at last persuaded because of the thrills involved. And the extra income.

But thrills had not come. Instead, the chore had grown dull. Guests came, usually by sea. They were odd, often. Usually they stayed overnight. Always they departed secretly, and she never saw them go. But that was all. And when Madame was in Paris, which could have been a bit more lively, the letter wasn't needed. Seemingly, Uncle Otto had other eyes for that period.

So the task had become dull, until now, with the extraordinary appearance of Mr. Summers, who wasn't a bit like the rest. Kate sighed, reached for her pen again. Mr. Summers was different and, for a while, she had hoped something might come of it. Corfu was a pleasant place, better if you could share it with the right kind of company. But Madame had flaunted her figure, flashed her eyes, turned on the charm, and that was the end of any hope Kate might have of getting to know Mr. Summers any better. Honestly, these French women! No delicacy at all! She sighed again, and began laboriously to write out the details.

Napoleon Solo struggled back to consciousness under the impression that his head was loose. He shook it to make sure, and the instant agony that came made him decide, firmly, not to do anything like that again for a long time. Levering his eyes open and focusing them against a strong glare, he saw he was looking along the top of a polished table littered with glasses and bottles. Beyond them, gradually hardening into outline and detail, he saw Countess Anne-Marie Louise de St-Denis. She watched him in calm appraisal, almost approval.

Easing back gingerly, he realized he was sitting in one of those stall-chairs again, but this one had improvements in the shape of a pair of chrome-steel bands that folded out from the armrests to pinion his wrists. He tried to stir his feet and assured himself there were more fetters on his ankles. He was caught. Moving his head carefully, he saw that Thrush was in full attendance, four pairs of bleak eyes being steadily fixed on him.

He forced his face into a thin smile, looked back to the countess, and revised his opinion of her. She was still beautiful, but now he saw her beauty as the coiled deadliness of a lethal snake.

"Welcome, Mr. Solo," she said, with crisp assurance. The use of his name served to shock some of the fog from his mind.

"Some mistake," he muttered, after a false start or two. The inside of his mouth had been scrubbed with a coarse brush or steel wool. It took some effort to make it work. He swallowed. "Mistake. My name is Summers."

"Let us not waste time. I knew you from the first moment I saw you in my telescope. For years I have maintained a comprehensive file, with photographs and descriptions, of all the more active agents of U.N.C.L.E. You are Napoleon Solo, *n'est ce pas?*" She laughed, cast a flashing eye on her uneasy audience. "I am flattered that U.N.C.L.E. should this time send its best man. For me, Mr. Stanton was old. Easy. I dealt with him. I shall also deal with you, only better this time."

"You will kill him," Morales pronounced, with no question in his tone.

"Oh no, señor. That would be waste. I will use him."

"Good!" Klasser grunted. "That is the better way. Good specimens are not easy to get. May we observe?"

"But of course. That is my purpose, as you shall see." She turned her burning stare on Solo again. "You have been disarmed, and all your toys removed. If you try anything foolish, one of my friends will kill you, and that would be unfortunate. But, if you are prepared to be sensible, I will free one of your hands, so that you may join us in a glass of this wine—and listen while we talk. Choose!"

"I could use a drink," he admitted, and she rose, moved away to a far corner where she must have operated a switch of some kind, for the cuff slid back from his left wrist. Then she came near, filled a glass and put it within his reach. Then she went back to her seat, but remained standing.

Watching her, it took him a moment or two to convince himself that he was not dreaming, that he had not slipped back three thousand years of time. She had caught back her black hair with a white band of silk. Her only clothing was a similar white silk, a simple garment that started from a silver brooch at her right shoulder and hung straight as far as mid-thigh, all in one piece, with just a hole for her arm, on the right side. On the left it swooped away from her shoulder to her left hip, leaving her left shoulder and breast uncovered, and from hip to hem it was loosely laced with a cord that ended in a fringe tassel. The whole was genuine Ancient Greek, not the modernized compromise, and like the ancients, it was all she wore. Then his eye caught and fixed on the one jarring note, the metal bangle and strange attachments that hung from her wrist.

"Now!" she said, in the tone of a queen addressing a cabinet. "You will have heard rumors, stories, hints. On the strength of those you are here, believing or not. Now you will hear, and see, the truth. You have heard me talk about health and beauty. You have seen my statues. You think I am, perhaps, something of a fanatic. Perhaps I am, you shall see. But I ask you to think of this. The glorious Greeks said: *Mens sana in corpore sano.* We say that a healthy body and a healthy mind go together. Perhaps it is true. But what is a healthy body, a healthy mind? How do you define these? Years ago I decided to take a position that no one can argue. A *perfect* body, this can be defined. A perfect body is a body without flaw, yes? And—a perfect mind is a mind without thought!"

If she was looking for a reaction from him, Solo thought, she was disappointed. The Thrush quartet was silent for several seconds. Then Vassi stirred.

"I do not understand. A mind without thought is what? Blank?"

"Exactly. We spoil white paper when we write on it, but alas, we must write. Children write on slates, and then wipe them clean afterward. If we could do this with a mind, it would remain perfect, you agree?"

"And useless," Morales grunted. "Get to your point, Madame."

"I will. I will show it to you as it came to me. I am a cosmetic surgeon. I spend long hours repairing the deficiencies in people. I know they will go and do the same foolish things again. I despair, sometimes, of humanity. But an idea comes. A question. Why do bodies grow to be imperfect? What is wrong?"

Klasser snorted. "This is obvious, Countess. We must

live as the circumstances allow, and this is not a perfect world."

"Quite so." She gave him a white-toothed smile. "So I decided to try and grow a life in perfect circumstances. Without flaw. Adam!" She lifted a finger and the impassive Hercules strode forward to stand by her side. She paused for effect, then said, simply, "Here is my first success. My perfect man. I made him."

Solo stiffened as the idea spread in his mind. Cabari exhaled slowly and said, "You had a good subject for your repair work, Madame."

"Not repair," she corrected. "Do not try to evade what is obvious. I made this man. I grew him, from an original cell-section. Here, in my laboratory. My first one. It was not easy, the first time, but I have learned much since then. A perfect human and a perfectly empty mind!"

"But"—Klasser was spluttering to get his words out —"this is not to be believed! This man moves and acts in an intelligent manner. If without thought he would be a cabbage!"

"So he is, without my thought. Look!" She raised her wrist and let the glittering attachments swing for a moment in the light then chose one with a red identification-spot on it. "This is a miniature transmit-receive device. It is one of a pair. The other? Adam, bow your head!" The man loweered his head forward slowly and she put her fingers into the thick black hair, ruffling, before drawing one fingerful aside. They could all see a small round patch of bare skin less than half an inch in diameter. "It is in there. I will show you. Adam, sit down."

Solo watched in chill horror as the herculean body settled into a chair. The countess did something to the thing on her wristband and the statuesque shape sagged and became limp and lifeless.

"Now he is without thought," she said, very softly. "Now you shall see." It was grotesque, stomach-turning, to watch her lean fingers probe, and then produce from the top of that immobile head a tiny tube of glittering metal. She held it for them all to see.

"Not to bore you with technicalities," she said, "it is enough to know that this is inserted in contact with the pineal organ. From there it controls the brain from the inside. I discovered this almost by accident. I had grown my perfect form, but it was blank and without mind. How to teach it, to train it in the way I wanted? Like a child, first with words and then on to subtleties? I thought not. That way is to establish exactly the very thing I did not want, patterns and habits like ordinary people's. But if I could reach the brain from the inside—ah! . . . And I did. Gentlemen, I will not bore you with all my struggles, my mistakes. Let it stand like this. Adam is now asleep, passive, unconscious—call it what you like. If I replace this command-switch, so"—she did it deftly and stepped away—"he is unchanged but within my power. I can reach him with this." And she took the bangle-unit in her fingers. "I have trained him to obey certain very simple instructions, enough to make him useful to me. He is, you might say, programmed. By me. Strong, swift, unquestioning and utterly faithful." She touched her switch and the impassive giant sat up and moved away to stand by the wall at her command. Vassi started a strangled comment.

"A moment!" The countess stopped him imperiously.

"No more bush-beating. My offer is just this. How would you like such a servant? Think, my friends. To have one person utterly bound to you, absolutely reliable, totally faithful, unquestioning, to be trained in whatever way you choose, to obey you whatever you say. Think now!"

Solo let out a very ragged breath and his hand shook as he drained the last of the wine in his glass. The technicalities were as far beyond him as they were beyond the Thrush quartet, but the facts were undeniable. And the potentials immense. A robot. An android robot. The perfect slave.

"I cannot contradict, Countess." Klasser was having trouble with his voice. "I must believe that you have achieved this. But I have one question. You say you grow these perfect ones, in your tanks, and that itself is hard to believe. But—I accept it. Still, do you expect us to wait for what?—twenty-five years?—for these creatures to be grown?"

"You are a man of science, Herr Doktor. It is a pleasure to know that your mind is working. But wrongly, in this case. With my techniques for artificial nurture, you see, it is possible to accelerate the process. I could grow you a servant, a slave, to your own order —within six weeks! But I can do better, much better. You have not heard the half, yet. I said that Adam was my first. I have others. Regard now!"

She moved away to another wall, touched a switch that set a concealed light glowing, and Solo leaned forward, struggling at his bonds, as he saw what was on display. In a long niche in the wall stood a row of statues, very like those he had seen in the entrance-hall, but immediately different in that they were flesh-colored. They looked real, like people sleeping. Ten of them, all female, all breathtakingly perfect, superbly beautiful, they stood—then he looked again and saw that they leaned back slightly, all of them, against black velvet supports.

"Female!" Morales said, deep in his throat, swinging his gaze to the countess. "Why? Why not male, like that one?"

"If you insist, señor, I can grow you a man, certainly. But think. Think how precious a perfect slave will be. Completely trustworthy, reliable, utterly obedient—and so decorative! Someone to wait in patience on your every whim, to look after you. And think, also, that a woman can go where a man cannot, and is unlikely to be suspect. And you may train her just as you wish her to be. Think. In a moment you shall make your choice. If you do not wish one of these, who are guaranteed against defect, then we can come to some other arrangement perhaps. But now I wish to tell you of the most important thing of all. Come and be seated again, and listen."

When she had them seated once more she said, "You saw the unit that I plant in the brain. It matches one other, here. These units are provided for me by the United States military scientists, although unwillingly. Perfectly matched pairs, powered by body heat, but one is stronger than the other, is in fact master. I have the masters here, in each case." She shook her bangle. "Now, you can control and order your slave by training her to respond to your voice, your words. This works, but it is clumsy. Think, if you"—and she pointed her finger at Klasser—"for example, had a master-unit in your head, contacting the pineal, you would be in full control of your slave at all times, by thought. You could see through her eyes, hear through her ears, speak through her voice, command her mind, at all times."

Klasser stiffened, squirmed back in his chair. "You shall not drill a hole in my head! It is out of the question!"

"I expected you to be concerned, Herr Doktor. But, as you shall see, it is a simple and painless operation, taking no more than twenty minutes or so. I will do it now, for you to see, on Mr. Solo!"

He had seen this coming. He strained helplessly at his bonds as she moved around the table to come near him. From somewhere she had taken up a slim case, from which she now took a hypodermic, which she held expertly.

"You shall see. I will insert one unit into Mr. Solo's brain. From that moment he will appear to be normal, but will be *my* slave. It is my regret, of necessity, that I cannot perform this operation on myself, but I will be able to control him quite well. And use him. I have done it before. And then, gentlemen, you will be convinced!"

CHAPTER SIX

THE taxi fled down the Rue Hebert as if trying to qualify for the Monte Carlo rally. In the back, Illya Nikovetch Kuryakin ignored the speed. He had ridden in Paris taxicabs before. He had done many odd, uncomfortable and dangerous things before, but never had he felt about them as he did about this one. For some inexplicable reason a sense of doom had perched on his shoulder all through the operation, ever since he had parted from Napoleon Solo.

Not that he'd had much time for brooding. One week had been spent in saturating himself in technical information, then the next two weeks had kept him inside the Soviet Union. There he had been passing himself off as Boris Krasnin, a French-born Slav, a bio-medical technician with one foot almost outside the law. Three days in Moscow had been enough to create the necessary background, the rest of the time he had spent in Tashkent, at the undercover center of the Soviet shadow world of plastic surgery and crooked science. His life had been a fiction, but he had to smile, thinly, now as he realized how easily it could have been true. There was a vast untapped potential in his mother country for men who could mold and manipulate the external appearances, legally and otherwise. His pretended purpose had been to forge a link between centers in Tashkent and the notorious possibilities inherent in the Paris

center of St-Denis. It would have been terribly easy
to really do just that.

So on the surface the project had been easy, but there
were undercurrents that he had not cared for, signs that
meant, to his eye, a breaking down of the values that
had kept the Soviet Union going along a hard path.
The subtle demoralization of affluence was having its
effect there just as it was everywhere else. While he no
longer had any loyalties to the Soviet, he did have boy-
hood memories and a degree of fellow-feeling for the
Russians, and the prospect had chilled him.

Adding to his gloom was the need to create an appearance. By habit he could be comfortable with a degree of untidiness, but that was not enough. People had
certain fixed mental images about Russians, and he had
to do his best to live up to them. Furthermore, this
was no case for any painted-on disguise. A man who
intends to move among highly skilled cosmetic surgeons
needs more than grease-paint and facial putty to create
an impression. For three weeks he had not shaved, and
was now sporting a yellow wisp of beard disreputable
enough to satisfy the wildest imagination. In the same
period he had washed his hair regularly with a hard soap,
deliberately neglecting to rinse it properly. As a conse-
quence his hair was straw-yellow dull and spiky. He
wore a dark chunky sweater, a coarse-weave jacket
with a touch of fur at the lapel, hairy pants and high
boots. The overall effect was convincing, but highly
uncomfortable to one of his temperament. He preferred
to be non-conspicuous.

The taxi slowed, halted, and he scrambled out, dis-
missing his inner preoccupations and tensing himself
to match wits with the people in charge, here at St-

Denis Surgery-Cosmetique. From the outside, no one would have taken the dingy old building for a medical house of any kind, but once inside the funeral doors and into the lobby all was hygienic chrome and glass, plus efficiency. A lady receptionist advanced to take his card. She managed, without effort, to make her plain black dress look chic, as only a Parisienne can. After a glance she nodded, moved away, gesturing him to follow.

"*Venez avec moi, monsieur.* I will discover if M. Lafarge is free to receive you. One moment."

She went before him to a desk, touched an intercom button and spoke in a rapid undertone. Beyond the wall, in his luxurious paneled office, Managing Director Louis Lafarge hushed his very important guest with an apologetic palm and attended to the call. Nodding, he made a quick decision, then turned again to his guest.

"A thousand pardons, monsieur, but you will realize that business is business. If you will please retreat into the next room I will dispose of this matter very quickly and then we can talk more." The covering door had barely closed when a discreet tap at the outer door announced the receptionist.

She entered one pace, stood aside, and announced, "M. Boris Krasnin, from Tashkent. M. Lafarge."

"*Bon jour, monsieur!*" Kuryakin inclined his head, managed to convey the impression of a heel-click without actually doing it, and advanced over the carpet. "I believe you are expecting me?"

"Of course!" Lafarge beamed and made gestures, but his alert attention missed nothing of his visitor's appearance, or his faultless accent. "I have your dossier right here. Yvette! You will request Gerda to come to me, at once, please! Now, M. Krasnin. A seat? You would care for a cigarette, no? An aperitif, then? It is good!" He produced a bottle and poured busily while making conversation. "You will pardon if I seem naïve, but it is a strange thing to me that your people should be interested in our kind of work. After all, the Soviet Union has a great name for medicine and surgery, and the many inventions of all kinds. Yet you wish to do business with us?"

"It is not so strange. Tashkent may be just a name to you, monsieur, but think. That area is now Uzbekistan, a preferred name in the new regime, but it was once Bokhara, famous for arts, beauty, the bourgeois things. The spirit is still there, but driven underground. It is not healthy, nowadays, to want to be beautiful, or different. Yet people want it, and where there is a demand, there will be a supply."

"Quite so!" Lafarge nodded agreement. "That is one rule which does not change." He looked up as a tap on the door heralded an interruption. With a scowl he called out, "*Entrez!*"

The door opened to admit a lean, dark-haired woman whose face was set in a severe and suspicious expression. With no more than a glance at Lafarge, she advanced to where Kuryakin sat, brought her left hand from behind her back to thrust it in front of him, fist clenched.

"*Kak eto nazivayetsya po rooski?*" she demanded, and opened her hand to reveal a small gilt and red enameled tube.

"*Pomada dlya goob,*" he sneered. "Are you trying to trick me, madame? Or you, monsieur?" He turned to spear Lafarge with an icy blue gaze. "This was so

73

obviously prepared, to have this stupid woman brought here, and for her to ask me to give the Russian name for a lipstick. What are you trying to prove?"

Lafarge spread his hands and shoulders in an eloquent shrug. "It was no more than a precaution, M. Krasnin. I have to be sure. Identities and names are so easy to fake. The name Krasnin means nothing to me."

"Names seldom mean anything to anyone. In England, once, I knew a girl called Cecilia Duff, if you can believe that. It was her real name. So what have you proved?"

"Enough." Lafarge was humble. "You must realize that in this business one has to be careful. There are secret formulae and techniques. And spies. And you do not look like a surgeon, or a technician."

"What do I look like, a Cossack?" Kuryakin did not say Cossack, but used an idiomatic equivalent that had such shocking associations that Gerda, who knew it, sucked in her breath in outrage. He swung his sword-like stare on her again.

"Does that shock you, *polyak?*"

Gerda cringed. In addition to her outrage, to be called Polish was too much, especially as she was and had worked hard to conceal the fact.

"I am not a Pole!" she denied shrilly.

"Then you must learn not to neigh like one. Have you any more little tricks to perform?"

She glared at him, compressed her thin lips, ducked her head at Lafarge, then scuttled out, shutting the door after her. The managing director of St-Denis Surgery-Cosmetique made haste to repair the damage in relations.

"Please banish the whole unfortunate incident from

your mind, my dear M. Krasnin. It was terribly *gauche*. I apologize. Now, which particular field of cosmetic surgery are you interested in?"

They talked generalities for a time, but Kuryakin was still on his guard. Lafarge was no fool. It was instructive to see how his expression tightened at the mention of skull and head surgery.

"I cannot speak on that section, M. Krasnin. Madame la Comtesse is the expert on that. No doubt you will have the opportunity to speak to her in person some time soon. Now, perhaps you would like to see around the laboratories and surgeries? Good!" He touched an intercom and spoke briefly, then rose. "Yvette will show you the way. Our chief surgeon awaits you. I think you will be impressed, M. Krasnin."

With the visitor departed, Lafarge settled back in his seat to think. Illegal surgery is not the most active market in the world. A pipeline from Russia could easily bring in a flow of patients. Profits. Madame la Comtesse would be pleased! M. Lafarge was beginning to smile to himself as his banished guest came from the far room and stood staring down at him.

"You know who that character was you just entertained?"

"Of course. M. Boris Krasnin, of Tashkent—" Lafarge let the words die into uneasy silence at his very important visitor's headshake. "No?"

"Definitely not, my friend. That repulsive and scruffy character was none other than Illya Kuryakin. An U.N.-C.L.E. agent. One of their best."

"You are sure of this?"

"Absolutely positive."

Lafarge seemed to shrink. "An U.N.C.L.E. agent,

here? What could he want? What can they suspect? There will be a raid!"

"Take it easy, now, Louis. He's on his own, a loner. I know his ways very well. When you're working a charade like that you have to do it alone, to cut down the chances of a slip-up. As for what he's after, that doesn't matter much, not now."

"But it does! It matters a great deal!" Lafarge grew excited. "We do not want trouble, not that kind. We avoid publicity, always. He must be stopped. Eliminated!" And he reached for his intercom once more.

"Hold it right there! You say you don't want publicity, and I can understand that, but if you send some of your boys to tangle with him you'll get publicity that will turn your hair white overnight. He doesn't stop that easy. I know him that well. He is very good—or very bad—depending on your point of view."

"Then what shall I do? I do not want U.N.C.L.E. agents here!"

"Don't worry about a thing. You have the address of his hotel? All right, just treat him nice and let him go back there. I'll take charge from that point. You just leave it all to me. I can handle him!" And Napoleon Solo grinned evilly down at Lafarge. "Oh yes," he said confidently, "I know his ways. I can handle him!"

It was late that same afternoon as Illya Kuryakin shut the door of his hotel room after him and leaned on it wearily. He was thankful to be able to relax for the first time in many hours. His encounter with chief surgeons and technicians had gone very well but it had been a strain, and he was not looking forward to maintaining the pretense very much longer. He would have to find what he was looking for quickly. Just now, though, all he wanted was a rest. He glanced around the large barnlike room he had acquired, and liked it. As in so many of the old, large, expensive Paris hotels, this very top suite, called the *chambre de courier*, was an awkward and misshapen afterthought, but it had a certain charm, and a truly magnificent view.

He crossed to the window to study the far-stretching roofscape. Rising out of it like some fantastic island stood the gilt-wreathed dome of the Invalides. Up here, high above the luxury level, one felt like a beggar at the gates of a great city, in it but not quite of it. The feeling suited him very well. He shrugged off his jacket, moved to the bed, paused a moment to admire its brass-bound massiveness, then heaved up and stretched out on it, kicking off his boots and wriggling deep into the white counterpane. An idle moment like this was a rare treat and he savored this one as far as he could stretch it. Then, sighing, he got out his communicator and flicked it into action with a practiced finger.

"Overseas relay," he requested, and traced the impossible outline of a flower on the wallpaper while he waited for the link.

"Is that you, Mr. Kuryakin?"

"Yes, sir. No snags so far. The managing director and technical staff of St-Denis seem to have accepted me, after a bit of preliminary suspicion. I've had a general look over their facilities."

"Good beginning. Don't try to rush it."

"Couldn't if I want to. Their facilities are really extensive, and first-class. There was a lot I didn't see, and some that called for explanations that I didn't get.

They have four highly-qualified embryologists on the staff, for one thing."

"Indeed! But you saw nothing to account for the theft of the communication modules?"

"No, sir. They'd be easy to hide, and impossible to detect unless one was in use. Anything new from Napoleon, on the Corfu end?"

"Hmm!" Waverly sounded peevish all at once. "News, you say? I have had reports, of a kind. The last I had was three days ago, from Turin."

"Turin? What on earth was he doing there?"

"I wish I could tell you. All he would say was that he was on the trail of something important but with no time to tell me what. It is most irritating!"

Kuryakin grinned as he shut off his instrument. Waverly was sparing with emotive words. For him to describe a situation as irritating was the equivalent of a string of lurid curses from anyone else. And, to be sure, Napoleon's behavior *was* curious. He had been staring absently at his little communicator for some seconds before he noted something highly significant about it. Right on the pencil-type tip a tiny neon glowed faintly. Just before leaving U.N.C.L.E. Headquarters, Section Three had presented him with this modified communicator. Jeremy Cronshaw, the technician working on the problem, had explained: "If you're anywhere within a half-mile of one of those modules, if it's in use, you'll get a glow from the lamp. It's not directional, I'm sorry, but at least it'll tell you if you're warm."

And he was warm now. Unfortunately, half a mile was quite a lot of ground to cover. He lay quite still on the bed, warm in the blood-red glow of the setting sun, and wondered what was the best thing to do; indeed, if there was anything effective he *could* do. And, in the hushed silence, he heard a faint but unmistakable click from behind a door he had not as yet opened.

The bathroom! He had not bothered to inspect it, because he had tangled with French plumbing before, and it was hardly conducive to comfort. But he did know that there was only the one door. That click—another came as he was thinking—meant someone was in there who had no business to be there. An enemy.

He put away his communicator and drew his pistol, all in the one movement, then waited, eyes riveted on the door.

CHAPTER SEVEN

SITTING quite still and silent, never taking his eyes from the door, Kuryakin nevertheless flogged his agile mind to consider the implications. How, for one thing, had the intruder managed to get in. And then, why? Had he been spotted at St-Denis, or was this possibly just a common burglar? The difference could be crucial. The bathroom, most probably, had a skylight. That would provide ingress for a burglar. And if that was all, then the mere sight of the gun would be sufficient.

But if it wasn't as simple as that, if, for instance, this was a Thrush manifestation, the outlook was totally different. He saw the bathroom knob turn, slowly. Not as a burglar would do it, at all. If Thrush was on the other side, the next move was predictable. Ease the door off the catch. Jerk it suddenly open. Drop and attack from the floor level, possibly. Kuryakin kept absolutely still, ready to move rapidly when required.

The knob came to a standstill. The door eased open just a crack. Then, exactly as he had expected, it crashed all the way open from a kick. And nothing. The man out there was flattened alongside the doorjamb, tense and ready, probably hoping for a startled shot. So he knew this was no common burglar, but a highly trained operator.

There came a sudden blur of speed as a man sprang-pounced and landed all square with gun aimed. Kuryakin checked his trigger finger just in the nick of time.

"Napoleon!" he sighed. "That's no way to—" and only razor-sharp instinct impelled him to forget the words he had in mind, to jerk himself to one side in frantic haste. He catapulted from the bed to the floor as the gun in Solo's hand bucked and roared, shattering the silence of the room.

He hit the carpet, rolled, got to a knee, then hurled himself crazily under the bed to avoid another crashing shot. This time, as he went headlong, he was fractionally slow and the white-fire agony of impact shocked his leg. It needed that anguish to wipe out the last traces of doubt from his mind. If there were mysteries here, one thing was plain. Solo was intent on murder, and nothing less.

Kuryakin reversed his tracks, squirming like an eel, bobbed up by the side of the bed and snapped off a shot as Solo swung around. Part of his attention noted the acute difference in sound between his gun and the shots from Solo, even as he saw that his own snap shot had been a lucky one. It had struck Solo's gun and jarred it out of his grip. Now it fell, clattered on the wood floor beyond the carpet and skidded away into a far corner. It left the way for Kuryakin to stalk around the bed angrily.

"Hold it right there!" he ordered, limping painfully, but with the gun steady in his hand. "Just one minute. What—?"

He never got to finish his question. Solo snapped out of his momentary stillness into a vicious kick and backfall. The kick smashed Kuryakin's grip, sent his weapon flying. The backfall dropped Solo only just long enough for him to strike the floor, roll, and dive for his own gun. The Russian swayed back, wincing at the weight on his injured leg, then launched himself headlong on top of Solo. All his weight came down hard, and he grasped at once for a bone-breaking arm-lock, but his efficiency was impaired by a sense of un-reality. It was hard to believe, to accept, that this snarl-ing hard-eyed fury who now snaked out of the arm-lock and flung a vicious groin-kick at him was really Na-poleon Solo. And, more to the immediate point, if this was Solo, he knew all the tricks and how to use them.

For some frantic seconds they rolled and snarled over each other like a pair of animals too evenly matched to have any advantage over each other. Then one squirm-ing roll brought Solo's head up against the leg of the brass-bound bedstead, and Kuryakin seized the head by the ears and pounded hard. Solo wrenched strongly, kicked out, his shoe striking Kuryakin where the bullet had plunged into his leg, wincing the Russian into mo-mentary agony and the chance to break free. He was away at once, diving into the corner after his gun. Again Kuryakin plunged after him, got a grip on one wrist and hung on desperately. He knew he was failing. This was a killing pace, and he was losing blood. Grunting with effort, his gaze began to fog up, mag-nifying the dusk of the room. He felt Solo rear up power-fully, and all he could do was to hang on for very life.

Then Solo gave a tremendous wrench, tore his wrist free, and the effort sent Kuryakin reeling backward, to catch the back of his knees on the bed. Too late to stop himself falling, he went with it, flung himself all the way over in a backward roll, over the bed and to the floor on the far side. He landed heavily, gasped for breath, fought his way erect, and as his head cleared the bed level, he saw a blur of movement. He threw himself desperately aside. There was one more shattering roar from Solo's gun. The room filled with a great light, just for a moment, and then there was nothing at all but deep black darkness.

"Monsieur! Monsieur!" A cracked and quavering voice demanded his attention. He screwed his eyes open to peer up at the strained old face of a woman. She was in black, with lace edges to her apron. He remembered her dimly. The concierge. "You are alive, monsieur?"

"I think so," he mumbled, and accepted the loan of her arm to sit upright. His head thumped like a brass bell filled with mud. The old woman stared fearfully at him as he put delicate fingers to his head. There was a tender place at his temple and his fingertips came away red.

"The doctor has been summoned," she told him. "He will be here soon. It was an assassin?"

"Something like that. You didn't see him, I suppose?"

"Me? Praise be to heaven I did not. I was on the stair. I heard a shot, then another, and another. I remained still, and screamed. And I waited for some time, then screamed again. What would you? It is not good, to be shot. Then Jules came, with questions, and we waited a while more. All was silent. We opened the door and found you, like this."

Heavily deliberate steps crackled across the floor and an old man with a white moustache came to stand and stare down at him.

"He escaped, monsieur. Through the bathroom skylight and up. That was *formidable!* The window has not been opened since I can remember. Ah, the doctor comes now. Do you wish that I summon the police?"

Kuryakin had been thinking as hard as his aching head would permit. He declined this last offer.

"It would not achieve anything, would it? The man is away, and with no traces or description, what can we do? I also wish to leave very soon. I would rather not be delayed with many questions. You understand?"

He reached for his wallet to facilitate their understanding, and his fingers brushed a folded piece of paper that he had not noticed before. He put it aside, passed crackling bank notes to the staff, then seated himself on the edge of the bed to make the doctor's inspection easier.

"You were fortunate, monsieur," the medical man informed him, after the blood had been sponged away and the bleeding halted. "This much to one side"— he held a finger and thumb very close—"and you would never have needed a doctor again." Kuryakin thought that over carefully. It must have seemed to his assailant that he had been shot dead. And possibly it would be a good idea to let him go on thinking that. At the leg-wound the doctor looked grave, and shook his head.

"For that, you should be in bed for a week, at least. If it is not convenient here I can arrange an ambulance and hospital for you."

"That's all right. Just fix it so that I can travel. It will be cared for but I have a very important appointment to keep. Please?"

The doctor departed eventually and Kuryakin, while appreciating his professional skill, was glad to see the back of him. He needed time to think. The crisp memory of a grim, snarling and murderous face, dreadfully familiar, shook up all his preconceived idea-patterns. He reached for his communicator, then stared at it a long while before putting it back in his pocket unused. That was out. He recalled the defection of Frank Stanton, and the total revision of communication methods that had made necessary. Now Solo had gone bad too, with all the inside information he had. Kuryakin set his jaw hard. All at once he felt very much alone.

But there were other channels. He screwed his head around stiffly, to stare at the telephone and think hard, in an attempt to remember the proper routine. Then he rose and limped around the bed to get at it. On the way he saw a dark slim object lying along the edge of the carpet, easy to miss if the light hadn't caught it just right. He kept his eyes on it as he settled on the bed again, lifted the telephone from its bracket and asked for a LOUVRE number. In a while there came to his ear a male voice in a bad mood. Yes, it agreed, this was the UNCLE Carpets and Furnishings Emporium and Wholesale Dealers, but there was no one present at such an hour except himself, the nightwatchman, and what else would anyone expect? Kuryakin wasn't put off. UNCLE Carpets was the front for U.N.C.L.E. Paris in just the same way that U.N.C.L.E. New York had an innocent front office.

"You will please inform M. Raymond Boncourt that his elderly and very impatient avuncular relative wishes urgently to speak with him. *Il y a un situation tres desagreable.*" There was a click and a wait of approximately forty seconds, then a totally different voice asked, cautiously: "Volga?"

"Right. Seine?"

"*Oui!* 'Allo, Illya. Why the round-the-houses approach, *mon vieux?*"

"Because all other channels are dangerous. Very dangerous. Leaking."

"Oh! *All* the other channels? You are positive?"

"Confirm. It is very bad. The little Corsican has turned his coat."

There came an audible gasp of shock. "*Bleu!* That is very bad. And very hard for me to believe."

"Me too. I got shot, twice, finding out. I am most probably dead right now."

"*Comment?* Oh, I comprehend. You need a funeral cortege, yes?"

"Nothing elaborate. Just get me out of here fast. I have to get this sad news to Greatuncle as quickly as possible. What about flight times?"

"A moment!" The voice went along, came promptly back. "A flight leaving Orly in thirty-five minutes. That suit you?"

"That will do very well. Now bring on your ambulance and carry the body away."

With that fixed he racked the telephone and went to pick up the odd object he had seen. As soon as his fingers touched it he knew what it was, and that Solo must have dropped it in the struggle. To the innocent eye it was no more than a propelling pencil with an eraser. But that eraser served as cover for a very fine lens, and the clip was the trigger that operated the camera up to a maximum of twenty exposures on a cunningly arranged roll of micro-film in the barrel of the pencil. Kuryakin slipped the pencil-camera into his pocket and pondered a while. Then he recalled the folded slip of paper that he had felt in his pocket, and groped for it. He unfolded it very carefully, because the paper was extremely thin and opened out into a fair-sized sheet. It was an odd wiring diagram, not too well drawn, and at the first glance it didn't make much sense. Kuryakin scowled at it. There would be plenty of time, later, to puzzle out what it meant. His immediate problem was to account for its presence in his pocket.

A wild thought insisted on being present in his mind. Perhaps Solo had not dropped his pencil-camera by accident—but deliberately. And had added this enigmatic diagram at the same time. But why? It was tempting to believe that Napoleon was somehow playing both sides against the middle and acting some peculiar part, but there could be no doubt at all about his recent invasion. That had been intended murder.

Back in the office of M. Lafarge, Solo reported his success with a confident grin.

"Nothing to it. He gave me a fight, sure. I expected that. He was one of their best men. But not any more."

"You are absolutely sure?" Lafarge insisted.

"I didn't hang about for a medical report, if that's what you want. But I shot him. I was as close to him as I am to you now. He went down. I waited, outside, to see the doctor come, and go away again, shaking his head. And then the meat-wagon came, and went. And so did I. What more do you want? He's dead!"

"Very well!" Lafarge shrugged. "I suppose it is fortunate that you were here to spot him. But unfortunate that now we shall not do business with the Soviets. That would have been profitable. Alas. Now, about this other matter. For two days you will remain under cover. Then, it is all arranged: you will fly direct to Miami Base, which is in Coral Cables. There you will be met. You will collect one dozen more radio-modules. You will leave again, almost at once, but you will not return here. You will proceed direct to Corfu, to Madame la Comtesse herself. These are her instructions. You understand?"

Solo looked up from cleaning his pistol and snarled angrily. "You bet I understand. I already knew all that, Louis."

"But how could you? The orders are sealed, and private to me!"

"Never you mind how, but I know exactly what the countess wants from me, at any time. I just know." And he put up a hand to stroke the top of his head.

The little man with the busy steam-press in Del Floria's had to look a second time, and grin, before he was sure that it *was* Illya Kuryakin. The golden straggle of moustache and beard was bad enough, to say nothing of the bulky jacket and hairy pants, but what put the clincher on it was the rakishly askew circlet of white bandage around his head. The little man widened his grin, opened his mouth for a brisk comment, then met the glacial stare in those blue eyes and forgot entirely what he had intended to say. Instead, he manipulated the trap that released the dressing-room panel; and wondered in silence just what the hell Illya had run into this time.

A similar stifled twist of amusement showed on the lips of the pretty receptionist as she pinned a badge on Kuryakin's lapel.

"I'll tell Mr. Waverly you're on the way up," she said,

and her finger was on its way to the intercom automatically until he stopped her.

"You won't," he said coldly, "use that. You won't do anything at all until you hear directly from Mr. Waverly, which will probably be by telephone. This is emergency. The condition is black!"

He walked stiffly away from her, fighting the tendency to limp. His leg ached. His head hurt. But that was only the minor stuff. There was a fire in his mind that he could hardly wait to unload. For once in his uncertain career he had the dubious satisfaction of seeing Alexander Waverly completely surprised.

"Mr. Kuryakin! You should still be in Paris!"

"Let us hope that a certain interested group of people also think so, and believe that I am, permanently. Don't touch anything yet, sir. I have to report that Thrush has got Napoleon Solo. Alive!"

For a long breathless moment the lead-lined office crackled with an utter silence. Then Waverly sighed and sat back.

"Have they, indeed? Sit down, Mr. Kuryakin, you look weary." He took up his desk telephone, pressed a button on it, and spoke. "Miss—close all forms of communication to and from this office except this telephone line to you that I am now using. Then issue firm instructions to cease all out-going messages of any kind until I personally countermand that order. Is it understood? Good. Now, Mr. Kuryakin, I suppose I can guess what you mean by saying Thrush has got Mr. Solo, but I would prefer that you told me. In full detail, please."

The old man was a good listener. Apart from one early move, to reach out for a pipe to fondle in his sensitive old hands, he kept quite still. His leathery face remained impassive, his eyes downturned and half-closed, and he asked no questions until the account was complete. Then, "There can be no doubt it *was* Mr. Solo?"

"None at all. I had some doubts, myself, at first. It is possible to fake likenesses, to impersonate with care, but you can't fake the way a man moves, or handles himself in a fight. That was Napoleon, all right."

"Hmm!" Waverly sighed again. "May I see the exhibits you've brought?" Kuryakin dipped into his pockets while the old man took up his telephone. "Send Mr. Cronshaw along to this office at once, please!" At the reply, he added: "Advise him that it is to do with his new pencil-camera device, and to bring appropriate equipment."

He took up the pencil, put it down again, brushed his finger over the paper diagram, was about to ask a question when he saw the three extra objects lying to one side.

"Bullets?"

"Yes, sir. I thought it worthwhile to extract those that were fired in the room. We can compare them with the rifling-pattern of Napoleon's gun, which ought to be on file. I'm sure it was him and his, but it can't do any harm to confirm."

"Agreed. But these would at once confirm one thing, at least—that his intentions were lethal."

"That's what puzzles me, sir. I've tried to believe that he was playing some kind of trick, but hardly with real bullets. I'm afraid there is no doubt about it. He was out to kill me."

The words were not easy to say. Waverly nodded in

sympathy. He knew better than anyone just how close these two men had been. Kuryakin was something of an enigma to everyone, and Solo had managed to get closer to him than anyone else. Now that he had turned renegade, Kuryakin was, in a real sense, utterly alone.

Jeremy Cronshaw came briskly in, carrying a developer-projector outfit, and took up the camera-pencil without further word.

"This won't take more than a minute or two," he announced. "This is a fast developer film, in here. I'll be able to project it for you right away, soon as it's dry." His busy fingers made skillful movements under a black velvet shroud, then there was a hum as he switched something on. His sharp eyes wandered to the much-creased paper.

"What's the diagram, Illya?"

"I'm not sure. I studied it a long time, on the flight. It seems to be some kind of communication wiring, but badly drawn."

"It's a mess." Cronshaw sniffed and studied it. "Doesn't mean a thing unless you know what values to insert here and here. Could be a kind of transceiver, though. Without the power-source. Excuse me." He straightened as the humming stopped in his machine. After a few more dexterous moves, he requested the lights to be dimmed and switched on his projector, aiming the picture at a small screen on the wall. It took a moment to get the focus, then they all saw a foreshortened picture of a head, seen from a point about three feet above the forehead. By the hair, it was the head of a woman, but there was one small patch where the head had been shaven clean.

The next picture showed the same head, but where there had been a patch of bare skin, there was now a dark orifice.

"A cranal operation!" Waverly murmured. "At a guess this must be some work done by Countess Louise. The next picture, Mr. Cronshaw!"

This time the screen showed a chart similar to those hung up for the benefit of anatomy students. It was of the human head in outline and profile. An arrow pointed to a specific area of the skull, on the top of the head. The next picture was once more a head, but this time in full-face, and again the arrow pointed down at the top of the skull. One more picture, and this time both Kuryakin and Cronshaw leaned forward excitedly.

"That's the diagram again!" Kuryakin declared.

"Right!" said Cronshaw. "But this time the values are properly put in. And you know what?"

"I know." Kuryakin sighed. "It's that damned radio-module thing. Any more pictures, Jerry?"

"Soon find out." Cronshaw moved switches, but the rest of the film was blank. He switched off, restored the lights. Waverly blinked, then his face contorted in-to a frown.

"Have you two seen something I've missed?"

"I've seen it," Kuryakin said, very quietly, "but I don't know that I can believe it, entirely. Except that I re-call, now, while I was fighting with Napoleon, I had his head and was banging it against the leg of the bed. And he had a small, round bald patch, just where it would show in that film. Jerry, that module doesn't need a conventional power-source, does it?"

"No. It's designed to function from body-heat. I know

what you're thinking, Illya, but it's fantastic. You can't just stuff a thing like that into a man's brain!"

"Perhaps you can, at that. Could we have Dr. Harvey in here, sir? This is something she could pass an opinion on."

"Of course." Waverly took up his telephone again and gave the order. Then he gripped his pipe for a moment in bleak thought. "I believe," he said, "that I am guessing what you two are thinking. That somehow that woman has discovered a way of inserting one of those modules into a human brain in such a way that she can exercise remote control by virtue of the matching other. And you"—he looked at the Russian—"believe that Solo has one in his brain at this moment?"

"It would explain a lot, sir. If it's possible."

Susan Harvey came in with brisk professional step, took one keen look at Kuryakin and made instant and appropriate movements with her black bag.

"Hold it, Dr. Harvey." The Russian halted her. "You can look me over later. Right now we'd like you to see some pictures. Jerry?"

They waited until she had seen all the film and the lights were on again, then Waverly took up the thread.

"The suggestion is, Miss Harvey, that something could be, and has been, inserted into the skull of a living person in the manner shown. Would that be possible?"

She took her time before answering. "I would prefer time to look this up before being dogmatic about it, of course, but offhand I would say yes, it is possible. So far as surgery is concerned, the brain is a special case. It is not sensitive to pain, and large areas of it are apparently without function. Patients have survived extensive brain surgery, have had large areas of the brain removed, in fact, and been no different. In the case shown, the arrow appears to be indicating the pineal area. Virtually nothing is known about the function of the pineal organ. If it has a function at all, which is doubtful. In structure it resembles an eye. There is a persistent but quite unfounded supersition that it is a kind of 'third' eye. It has been believed, at various times, that it is through the pineal eye that the soul and body are joined. It's safer to say that we know very little about it, or what purpose it serves. As for inserting something in the skull just there, that would be simple enough. It would depend on the size and nature of the insertion, of course."

"The thing we have in mind," Kuryakin said heavily, "is about half an inch long and the caliber of an ordinary pencil-lead. It's a miniature transmitter-receiver, powered by body-heat."

"In its military usage," Cronshaw added, "the man in the field would have it taped to his jawbone so as not to interfere with his movements. It's designed to convert into audio-frequencies."

"That's rather beastly." Susan Harvey repressed a shiver. "I suppose someone with that thing in his head would hear voices."

"He would hear commands. Instructions," Kuryakin declared, with sudden inspiration. "And he would obey, or suffer. Imagine what a simple power-boost would do! And the person at the other end, the controller, would be able to listen in and hear everything that went on, all the time!"

"Well"—Waverly sighed and put down his pipe—"at least we know this much, then. Mr. Solo is in the hands of the enemy, but not willingly. He is under compulsion by this fiendish device. The next question must be, how do we get him back?"

CHAPTER EIGHT

As the whole of the efficient organization that was U.N.C.L.E. seethed into fervent activity to deal with the problem, Waverly was at pains to make one point clear.

"We want Mr. Solo back," he said, facing a team of experts from all sections, "preferably. But failing that, he must be killed. He is much too dangerous to be left in that woman's hands." It was a bitter decision and there was more than one sympathetic glance for Illya Kuryakin, but no one questioned the correctness of it. The United Network Command was too important to be risked for the sake of one member.

For two days, Kuryakin did less than anyone. Try as he might, his brain was too bothered by various factors, and in any case he was in urgent need of rest and recuperation from his wounds. Susan Harvey attended him as often and regularly as her time would allow, but he was difficult, both as a patient and as a person. In neither valence would he render any clues as to his feelings. Never, she felt, had she made less impression on a man. It was as if she were transparent, as if he couldn't see her, no matter how carefully she tried to make herself pleasant and attractive. He had interest in two things, and two things only. One was for news that Solo had been sighted. The other was for some outcome to the ceaseless quest for some efficient way of getting that telltale module safely out of Solo's head, if and when they did manage to catch him.

Answers to both came in quick succession on the evening of the second day. Kuryakin had taken up residence in one of the spare small apartments within the crumbling brownstone facade, so as to be on hand in the event of any news. Susan Harvey had come to visit him, ostensibly to change his bandages but in secret fact to try out on him the effect of her newest and most brief minidress. She had long and extremely attractive legs, and she knew it. He would have known it too, had he taken the trouble to look, but he didn't. She sat, now, directly opposite him and crossed her lovely legs with deliberate abandon. Then she sighed and shook her head in despair.

"All right!" she declared. "I'll tell you!"

"Hmm?" He sounded indifferent. "Why?"

"Jerry Cronshaw made me promise not to, because it's still in the uncertain stage, but he thinks he is getting close to a way of jamming the output of those modules with a directional beam."

"Hah?" Kuryakin sat forward at once. "That's more like it. If we can catch him, and jam the signal effectively until we can get him operated on—the operation is straightforward enough, isn't it?"

"Nothing to it," she declared. "I can do it myself."

"That's great!" The change in him was startling. She felt a twinge of sharp envy that he could care so much more about his friend than he did for a woman—meaning herself.

"He really means a lot to you, doesn't he?"

"It's not that, ex: ctly." His grin was instantly wry. "It's just that he's not safe, running around on his own, and with that radio-voice inside his head there's no telling what he might get up to."

"Oh well." She took courage from his flippancy. "If you're feeling that much better, how about going out somewhere this evening, to celebrate?"

"Celebrate what?" he asked pointedly. "The redundancy of female attire? You can't surely be serious about going out in that?"

"Why not?" she demanded, tugging ineffectively at an almost nonexistent hem. "What's wrong with it?"

"There isn't enough of it to be wrong. You'd be arrested!"

"All right!" She shrugged. "We'll stay in and celebrate, then . . ." Her suggestions trailed off as the telephone shrilled for attention. Waverly's voice came.

"Mr. Kuryakin? Is Dr. Harvey with you? Good. I want both of you in my office, at once, please."

"Is it Napoleon?"

"I think so."

"We're on our way!"

Waverly's outer office was full of silent grave-faced attentive men. Number One, Section One, waiting until the new arrivals were settled, swept them with a steady gaze.

"The wheels are beginning to turn," he announced. "Last night another military center was raided and another consignment of the radio-modules was taken. This time we have had instant cooperation from the military as to critical wave-lengths, and those modules will be useless to whoever has them. That is by the way. We *know* where they are. At this moment they are being held within Thrush-Miami headquarters. Our man on the inside informs us that the Thrush station is standing by for an important courier from Paris, who is to collect the modules and carry them to Corfu. We believe we know who that courier will be."

He swiveled to snap his fingers and the display screen lit up to show detail of a rambling old house in Coral Gables, standing in semi-tropical grounds.

"If it's Solo, we are going to have one hell of a job snatching him out of that rat's nest," a deep voice declared.

"That is not the intention, here. If, as I think, it will be Mr. Solo, our strategy will be to let him enter, make his pickup, and leave again. We will take him later. A point to stress. This operation must be done with great care. For one thing, we must operate completely outside our customary style, in a completely unorthodox manner, because we are dealing with a man who knows all our routines. For that same reason we cannot afford to use anyone who is known to him by sight."

"That won't work!" Kuryakin objected instantly. "Napoleon knows just about every enforcement agent on the staff. All the top-rank men, anyway. If we pull out all of them we might as well quit right now. We'll be so crippled, we won't stand a chance!"

Waverly half-closed his eyes, stroked his jaw with his pipe-stem as he weighed the objection, then shrugged in resignation.

"Very well, we will have to make do with very careful and elaborate disguises. Now for the essential strategy. I'll sketch it, and if anyone can suggest improvements, please interrupt as we go. We have very little time to waste."

Napoleon Solo sat back in the taxi, apparently quite

at ease, but in fact very much on the alert. The pickup operation had gone very smoothly, just a trifle too smoothly for his peace of mind. Surely there should have been *some* sign of opposition? The cab crossed the Tamiami Canal, and once again he could see the airport lights.

"I'm certainly sorry I couldn't stay awhile and visit with you boys," he said. "You seem to have a nice place here. In the daylight, they tell me, the scenery is pretty good too!"

"The way I heard it," one of his escorts chuckled, "the scenery is kind of outstanding where you're going, too. They say the countess is a real dish! What's your word?"

"I'll tell you." Solo grinned. "You take Helen of Troy and the Queen of Sheba. Then you add in those two Italian lulus, Gina Longname and Sophia. Then Brigitte Bardot, the best parts of Jayne Mansfield and Liz Taylor. Stir and save the cream, and you aren't even close!"

"I don't wonder you're in a hurry to get back. How's about asking us all out there for a vacation, sometime?"

"The expenses come high, but I'll give it a mention."

The cab swayed, slowed and halted. The small group climbed cautiously out and looked around.

"This is too easy," one of them muttered, as they formed an apparently casual but efficient surrounding escort for Solo. "I was half-hoping some of your U.N.-C.L.E. buddies would want to horn in. They must be slipping!"

"Just goes to show!" Solo made a throwaway gesture. "Without me—nothing! I bet they don't even know I'm here."

No one offered to call him on the wager. The little party halted at the edge of the landing field.

"This is it," said the man in charge. "Our job is to see you on the plane, that's all. And there it is!"

"Right!" Solo kept his grin, squeezed down on the sudden tension that gripped him, and made a goodbye gesture. "See you again, sometime."

He set away to walk across the open space. His eyes were constantly moving. He saw nothing suspicious. Neither did his sharp-eyed escort. They were not meant to. But he had instincts, and they were tickling him now. Nor were they false. Ever since landing he had been carrying, unwittingly, three unobtrusive electronic bugs, planted on him by disguised agents. From that moment, attentive monitors had listened in on his every word and, by cross-reference, had been able to pinpoint his location at all times.

Those three "fingers" pointed unerringly at him now as he dawdled across the open, so as to be the last passenger aboard. In this moment the haunting, echoing, nightmare "voice" in his head was mercifully silent. He knew "she" was there, though. He had never been able to forget it, right from the moment the needle had first entered his skull. Silent, painless, yet in some uncanny fashion always there, like a never-ending tension in his head.

He was almost to the gangway now, and no one anywhere in sight. The last straggle of passengers had vanished into the dark doorway up there. He swept one last glance around, wishing his nerves would ease off a little. It was hard to be easy and nonchalant when every instinct he had was screaming a warning. He mounted the tread and ran lightly up the slope, pausing at the top to turn and wave to the watchers he couldn't see but knew were there. It was done. He had made it. He turned to step inside.

A slim, very erect figure moved out of a side door and stood facing him, obstructing the way. A man all in black, even to the jet-black hair and mephisto-phelean beard. Only the blazing blue eyes and chill grin remained to give him away. Solo stopped as if he had walked into a concrete post. Ice touched his nerves.

"You!" he gasped, and in that second an infernal buzz-ing started up in his skull, making him cringe, blurring his vision. "You!" he croaked. "But—I shot you, didn't I? In Paris?"

"So you did, Napoleon." The familiar voice came cold and firm over the hellish racket in his skull. "So you did. And now it's my turn!"

Solo snatched for his weapon, but it was also his turn to be too late. The pistol in Kuryakin's fist spat once, and Solo felt the pang, right in the middle of his forehead. It spat again, but he never felt that one at all. He sagged slowly forward, unseeing and uncaring. Kuryakin caught him gently, settled him over one stur-dy shoulder, turned and went, heavy-footed, to where the aircraft's emergency escape hatch stood gaping open ready. It was on the far side of the cabin from the watchers. To the pop-eyed passengers he offered a genial grin.

"It's quite all right, folks. This is only a film sequence for a T.V. show. Won't keep you more than a minute. Fun, isn't it?"

Beyond the open hatch, down there on the concrete, stood a pickup wagon, all ready. A couple of husky agents stood on its roof. They reached up for the Russian's limp burden, lowered it gently down and inside, then made room for him to jump down himself. Seconds later the wagon rolled away, swiftly and silently, to a far corner of the airfield. There a charter plane stood, propellers clicking over. Ten minutes more, and the plane was airborne over Hialeah and heading north.

CHAPTER NINE

PART of the aircraft cabin had been set aside as an emergency operating room. Solo lay inert on the narrow bed as Susan Harvey checked his pulse and respiration and announced herself satisfied. Waverly and Kuryakin were standing anxiously by.

"It's going to be all right," she said. "You planted the anesthetic darts just right, Illya. He'll be ready in a moment or two."

"You'll be able to locate the exact spot of the insertion?"

"No trouble to that, Mr. Waverly. Here, you can see for yourself." She lifted the unconscious man's head and showed where a small flap of skin and hair could be lifted up easily. "Plastic plug in place. I doubt if I'd have to use instruments, other than a small pair of forceps. Still, I'll scrub up and do it thoroughly."

"All right." Kuryakin sighed and relaxed a shade. "I'll go and get this comic-opera makeup off." He ran fingers through the caked dye on his hair and made a face.

"I rather like it dark," she said. "It suits you!"

He glared at her, but the words which came to his tongue were hardly suitable for saying aloud, so he swallowed them and went limping away to the aircraft's tiny washroom. Waverly lingered, but his thoughts had gone far beyond the operation.

"You anticipate no difficulty in removing this gadget from Mr. Solo's brain, but can you give any estimate as to whether it might have produced any permanent effect?"

"That's something I won't be able to say until we've had a full-scale check-up. Not until we get back to a proper laboratory. The possibilities are immense, and I've nothing at all to go on. Most obvious, of course, is the risk of infection, but I imagine the countess would be too good a surgeon to make that kind of mistake. There may, also, be localized brain damage. Most probable, I would say, is some kind of mental disturbance, and that is quite outside my field."

"I see. Thank you for being candid, Miss Harvey. I'll leave you now to do what you must. Keep him under sedation until we can lay on a proper checkup."

Waverly went away to his cabin, there to activate a radio-link which disturbed a quiet, urbane-looking man who was at that moment leaning back in a seat in the very aircraft Solo had been booked to fly in. At the faint bleat of his communicator he stood up and made his way briskly to the washroom, there to pull out his instrument and answer.

"Crawford White here."

"Everything went as planned, Mr. White. You know what to do now. When you change planes in Rome you will be bothered by the Rome police, you will make a break, escape from them, and then go to ground. It has all been prepared. You will be Mr. Solo until you receive a further order from me."

"I have all that, Mr. Waverly."

"Good. You may now remove the lead-shield from your module and go ahead as planned. No more communication with us by this channel. Be alert for signals from Corfu, and reply accordingly. Out!"

Whereupon Crawford White carefully deactivated his communicator so that it would not sound again, then, with equal care, set about peeling off a protective layer of lead-foil from the module that was securely fastened to his jawbone by adhesive tape. It was no coincidence that he looked very like Napoleon Solo in appearance, nor that his voice was very similar in tone. He had been selected with those very characteristics in mind. He was about to become Solo in everything but the fact. It was highly important that Countess Louise did not discover that her tame dog had shed his leash. It was all part of a plan that Waverly had concocted, one that required Solo to put his head back into the mouth of the tigress once again, just as soon as it could be established that he was sound in mind and body.

There were minor details to clear up. The stolen modules had been recovered and were even now being inspected by a team of experts under Cronshaw. The jamming interference was off, but could be restored at the least sign of consciousness in Solo. And Crawford White's module was an exact harmonic match for the one in Solo's head. Waverly scanned through a long list of such lesser items, ticking them off. A lot of work had gone into this operation. Harmless copies of the modules were already made and standing by for the next step. Waverly chewed on his pipe and reviewed his plans over and over, striving to find some weakness in them. It was the only thing to do, now, until Solo had been checked out. On him rested the final action.

Chores done, his musings turned to a slightly different theme. There seemed to be a fairly firm and unbroken chain of effect from the theft of the radio-modules, then to Countess Louise, and to this devilish device for controlling a person like a puppet. But how did this concern Thrush? If there was a logical tie-up, Waverly couldn't see it. The countess was definitely involved with Thrush, of that he was certain, although he didn't know just how she functioned within that vast, faceless and sinister organization.

But how on earth could the ability to implant a radio-control unit inside a person's skull have any great attraction for the evil men whose one aim was to dominate the civilized world? It was tempting to think they had some wild idea of surgical implantation for large numbers of people, but that just was not feasible. In the first place there weren't all that many modules available. Even the non-profit resources of military research couldn't make them in very great quantity. And in the second place there was the surgery to think of, and the complex of control equipment. The idea just would not work.

Waverly shoved away from his temporary desk and went impatiently away to find Kuryakin and argue it out with him.

The small, three-bed ward was hushed and quiet. Waverly and Kuryakin stood near, but not too near, the bed where Solo lay unconscious. Two male agents chosen for bulk and muscle lounged unobtrusively but alert in the far corners. Susan Harvey stood by the bed, holding one limp wrist and nodding to herself in satisfaction.

"Almost ready," she said, moving briskly to the trolley where instruments stood ready. She took up a hypodermic. "The sedation is almost gone. This should wake him up right away. I can't tell you exactly what to do in advance, because I don't know what's going to happen. The only advice I can offer is to stay calm, try to reassure him if he seems to need it, and don't use violence unless it is absolutely necessary. Now!" She went back to the bedside, made the injection swiftly, then withdrew a little, to stand and watch like the rest.

The man on the bed stirred, rolled his head, sighed heavily, then opened his eyes. He stared at the roof, then his eyes came sideways, saw Susan, focused on her. He broke into a strained smile.

"I know this bit," he said, in a voice dusty from long disuse. "I'm supposed to say, where am I?"

"Who are you?" she asked, in counter-question, and his smile dimmed.

"You have a point. I am Napoleon Solo, late of the United Network Command—" He stopped suddenly, a curious look on his face. He shook his head, but not as a negative, more like a man who expects it to hurt and is wondering why it doesn't. Susan Harvey made a guess.

"You're all right now," she said. "It's gone. I've taken it out." And she made a slight gesture to the top of her own head. Solo stared and the struggle to believe her was apparent in his face. Then relief, a visible sag and audible sigh of relief.

"I don't know who you are, or how you knew, but I owe you much. To have that damned twitch, that infernal subaudible whisper, gone! It's been a kind of refined hell to know that at all times, no matter what I did, she was listening, right there inside my own head. . . . You're sure?"

"Oh yes, quite sure. Several hours ago. You are safely back inside U.N.C.LE Headquarters now, Mr. Solo. I am Dr. Harvey, of the resident medical staff."

"I'm glad to meet you. I wish it could have been under happier circumstances, or sooner. Right now I have to report to Mr. Waverly. It's urgent!"

"Look around," she invited, and moved back a step. Solo hoisted up on an elbow and moved his head.

"Mr. Waverly!" He inclined his head a fraction, then grinned as he saw Kuryakin. "You too, Illya. I'm glad to see you can stand being shot. I've been trying to forget that bit of nightmare for some time. Was I dreaming, or did you shoot me, just a while ago?"

"No dream. But those were anesthetic darts, for a purpose. Yours were real bullets, Napoleon!"

"I know." Solo compressed his jaw sadly. "I didn't have much choice. I tell you, you've no idea just what brainwashing is until you've had a she-devil actually sitting inside your skull repeating her commands. It's enough to drive a man mad."

"Did it succeed, Mr. Solo?" Waverly's voice was quiet but firm.

"I don't think so, sir, but I'm ready to take any tests you like. In the meanwhile, there's something you need to know." He sat up in the bed now, threw back the sheet and swung his legs to the floor. The beefy agents moved closer, just in case, but he never even noticed them. "Louise is setting up one of the most deadly rackets you can imagine. You know, I take it, how the modules work?"

"Not exactly." Waverly was curious but very much on his guard.

"It's really very simple. Louise explained it all to me when I was in no position to argue. You see, she kept one half of the module pair to act as command. That's fitted into a power-transmitter with a microphone. There are various settings. On one certain setting she can talk into my head and I can't hear at all, not consciously. It's pitched subliminal. It's deadly!"

"Not any more," Susan reminded him, and he gave a quick laugh.

"It's going to take me a while to adjust to that again. Now—to get at the real devilment. With those modules Louise was experimenting with the remote control of various creatures, so I gather, but her big aim was to enslave people. She grows people." He said it flatly, waiting for the reaction. It took a while to come, and him some time to explain.

"You mean"—Susan's voice shook as she tried to appear scientific—"that woman can actually grow complete human copies? Androids?"

"That's exactly it. And perfect, they are. Beautiful. But brainless. No, not brainless, that's not the word. Mindless. Just waiting to be trained. As she puts it, an empty book, waiting to be written in."

"That doesn't entirely surprise me," Kuryakin put in, quietly. "I saw those laboratories, in Paris. You will recall, Mr. Waverly, I reported that there were embryologists on the staff. You can see why, now."

"Good heavens!" Waverly caught his breath. Solo grinned.

"Seems like a dream now, Illya, but that was some

scrap we had. But I did shoot you, surely? I remember that bit."

"You missed." Kuryakin moved forward, shoved his fringe aside to show the almost healed scar. "I've told you a hundred times, Napoleon, that you tend to pull off to the right with that Luger of yours in a snap shot."

"Yeah!" Solo shook his head ruefully. "I'll have to watch that."

"This is no time for badinage—" Waverly began, testily, but the Russian halted him with a gesture.

"Just a minute, sir. Napoleon, did you drop that pencil-camera by accident? Really?"

"No. I planted it. And the diagram, as best I could. It wasn't too easy to get those pictures, let me tell you, but that fiendish woman has to sleep sometime."

"You did very well, Mr. Solo. Please go on with your account. You spoke of a master-plan?"

"That's right, sir. On the surface, it sounds like nothing. Louise is selling slaves, of her own make. She guarantees to deliver the perfect slave, servant, assistant, companion, call them what you like. At a price. A quarter of a million dollars each, cash on the nail. Each one fitted with a skull unit, the matching half of which is supplied to the new owner."

"That is certainly gruesome." Waverly shivered. "But not a very great threat to us. Is it?"

"Not, as I said, on the surface. But there's more. So far she has made her sales pitch to the various regional heads of Thrush. And she has managed to con them into a further refinement. She operates on them, just as she did on me, and inserts a command module to match the slave module. The con is that the big Thrush now has a perfect slave, utterly obedient and absolutely reliable, that will respond to the master's every wish, be in total contact at all times, and through which the master can literally 'be' wherever the slave is. The ideal snoop."

"Just a minute!" Kuryakin became agitated, and Solo grinned.

"You've spotted it, Illya. You would, I guess. It's like this, sir. What Louise is *not* telling them, but I happen to know, is that she has her own split-frequency radio setup. She can, at will, transmit into or listen from *any one* of those modules, at any time. Not only does she plan to be on the inside of everything that happens within Thrush, she plans, in the long run, to take over Thrush, from the inside!"

"Can she do that?" Waverly demanded.

"I'll say. When the little demon inside your head starts to shout, you obey. Believe me, you obey, or you get a jolt that feels as if the top of your head is coming off. She can do it!"

CHAPTER TEN

OUT of a long and tense silence, Waverly spoke with a sigh. "At any rate we have established one thing to my satisfaction, Mr. Solo. Your mind is unimpaired. That is something to be thankful for. But your news is very bad indeed. I need hardly point out to any of you that the one thing which has always been on our side is the human tendency among the Thrush Hierarchy to quarrel among themselves for supremacy. It is their one weakness. And they know it as well as we do. That is why they have labored so long to perfect their Ultimate Computer. Of course, it goes against the human ego to take orders from a Computer, which is still a point in our favor. But if this dreadful woman gets her way, we lose all that. The entire Thrush evil will come under the single-minded and brilliant control of one person. That we must stop, at all costs."

"That means stopping Louise," Solo declared. "There's no other way. And I don't see how. Not now. If I was still on the inside, I could get close enough—but that's out, now. You can safely bet that she knows, by now, that I'm off the chain. Free of her influence."

"That is not necessarily so, Mr. Solo." Waverly dropped the words into the discussion very gently. Solo stared.

"But she must know. Just as soon as you took that thing out of my head, it would go dead, and she would know!"

"At this moment," Waverly said, as if talking to himself, "Mr. Crawford White is on the plane you were supposed to catch. When he touches down at Rome there will be a carefully contrived conflict with the Rome police. He will run, will go into hiding, and stay under cover until the heat is off."

"So?"

"So Mr. White bears a strong physical resemblance to you, Mr. Solo. In particular his voice is very like yours. At times, for the amusement of fellow-agents, he has been known to do lifelike impersonations of you. *And* he has a module taped to his jaw that is a perfect wave-length match for the one we removed from you."

Solo thought hard, and it was obvious that he didn't like what he was thinking.

Waverly waited a moment then resumed: "He will remain in hiding long enough to give us time to work out some feasible plan for removing that menace from Corfu. We have two or three days, possibly more. But, and I am sure you have already realized this, Mr. Solo, the success of any plan we may devise will depend to a great deal on you. In the circumstances I feel I cannot order you to cooperate. I cannot order you to put yourself in jeopardy again, where that woman is concerned. But I can, and I do, ask you to consider our plan."

Solo's face was a study in tension, but before he could bring himself to pass comment, Susan Harvey stepped into the discussion.

"Mr. Solo is still my patient," she stated firmly. "I forbid any further discussion or planning for at least twenty-four hours."

"That's it!" Solo caught her up quickly and grinned. "Doctor's orders. You can't argue with those." He looked up at her, then up and down, and his grin bloomed into a warm smile. "Especially a doctor like this. All at once I feel weak and helpless. Leave me!"

Kuryakin snorted. "You need a doctor like you need a hole in the head!" He aimed a cold blue stare at Susan. "Don't let that helpless-in-bed routine fool you. What you should have done, while you had the chance, was to have inserted an on-and-off switch into his skull. You may need it." He moved to the door on the heels of Waverly and the two grinning agents. In the doorway he halted and turned.

"Don't worry, Napoleon," he said. "I won't tell anybody."

Solo bit it. "Won't tell anybody what?"

"That you really do have a hole in your head, as they have always suspected!"

He ducked out of the door as Solo reached for something to throw, and then chuckled easily. But the smile faded as he turned to look at Susan.

"It's a point," he murmured. "Will I be affected, do you think?"

"Not at all," she assured him. "In a week or two there'll be hardly a trace. With all her faults, *Docteur-Proffesseur* Louise Santelle is still a fine surgeon. She made a neat job."

"Who?"

"Your Countess Louise. I looked her up in the medical records. She was a brilliant woman in her field. Too bad she had to go crooked."

"Ah well," he sighed, and wriggled happily in the bed. "Let's not talk about her. Let's talk about you. How come, for instance, that someone as beautiful as you has been right here in Headquarters all this time and I didn't know?"

"I can't imagine," she retorted calmly, "since my special field is dealing with the worst cases of infection and contamination."

"Like that, are we?" he murmured. "Tell me, what will your baby sister say when she finds out you've stolen her best dress?"

"I think," she said, "it's high time I gave you another shot of sedation. You're beginning to get worked up. . . ."

The trim blue-and-silver yacht heaved lazily at her anchor in the jewel-blue swell of the Ionion Sea, just half a mile south of the Kanoni Lagoon, and slightly less than that away from the eastern shoreline of the island. On the upper deck, in the glorious afternoon sunshine, Illya Kuryakin lolled in blue bathing briefs and acted the part of a careless vacationer. By his side sprawled Susan Harvey, taking the sun in a minimum white bikini. The pair of them had gone deliberately through the charade of showing excitement and interest in the scenery, had stared adequately but not too pointedly at the pink-and-white fairy-tale palace in the near distance. Now they were just lazing, showing no great interest in anything.

Solo had warned them about Louise and her habits with her telescope, so they knew they had to go through with the act thoroughly. Their detailed and critical study of that cotton candy edifice on the shore had been done from the safe obscurity of below decks. Down there, too, were four men, agents hand-picked for muscle and determination. They were keeping completely out of sight. They were ready and willing to cross that blue water and pitch into any activities, if called for, but not otherwise. Waverly had hammered that point home repeatedly.

"We can expect no local cooperation or support," he had warned. "And we do not want to provoke an international situation. There are plenty of people who would be only too happy to be able to pin on us the idea of an invasion by force. Hostile power. Interference in national affairs. That kind of thing. The countess is a well-known and respected figure. She would make full use of any such excuse, given the ghost of a chance."

So care was essential. Everyone understood that. The one thing none of them discussed, nor doubted, because it was so obvious, was that to Solo had fallen the hardest job of all, one with the most desperate risk. Desperate, and highly delicate, Kuryakin mused as he rolled over, and looked at his wristwatch.

"His plane is due to touch down in half an hour," he murmured. "Right on sunset. The Thrush big boys have been there almost an hour. She will be giving them the first sales pitch by now, and anxiously waiting for him with the new supply of modules. It's going to be tight. You sure he's o.k.?"

"Of course I'm not sure," Susan retorted, the edge on her voice revealing her tension. "I've said all along that he should have had at least another week under observation and therapy. But you said we couldn't spare the time."

"Don't blame me, blame the circumstances," he said. And it was true.

As Solo had pointed out himself: "I'm overdue. I was instructed to fly direct to her from Miami, and the longer I'm delayed the more suspicious she is going to get. I know we have a cover-story prepared, but that's too thin to be stretched very far."

And there had been another spur to speed. Keen-eyed observers had reported all the signs of another gathering of the big Thrush people at the cotton candy palace. The reason was obvious, as Waverly had pointed out.

"The countess works out her operations very careful-ly. Obviously this meeting follows on the acquisition of a new set of modules and is the moment for more sales. And each one of those sinister delegates will be carry-ing a quarter of a million dollars in cash. This is a moment that might not come again in years. We have to seize it."

So the plans had been worked out and set in motion at top speed. Solo had been able to help a great deal with inside information. He had been supplied with fake modules. He had described, as precisely as he could, the electronic setup, and the yacht carried equip-ment to jam any frequency the countess might use, as a last resort.

But, as Solo had been able to warn ahead of time, "Be careful how you go, if you have to break in. That palace is booby-trapped like nothing you ever saw. Louise has it stuffed from floor to roof with priceless art treasures, and she takes no chances with them."

He reviewed that, and other things, as he sat in the plane and stared down at the green and blue beauty of the island now spinning and turning below as the pilot wheeled to get into position for the run-in. Just barely, he could see the yacht properly in position. He slid a hand into his pocket to get out his communi-cator and murmur into it.

"Puppy-dog to Goldilocks. Any bumps?"

"Not a wrinkle, so far." The reply was prompt. "The birds are gathered safely in. I shall go swimming at dusk. Shine blue when you need me. Good luck, and out!"

Solo carefully deactivated his instrument and put it away. In the same movement he peeled a thin strip of lead-foil from the module that was stuck to his jaw-bone with flesh-colored plastic, knowing that Crawford White, who was one of the strong-arm party below, would be simultaneously removing his module. So far as they could tell, Louise had not detected the switch at all. He hoped she would not detect this second one. He eyed the red warning in front of him and spoke it aloud, ruefully.

"Fasten your seat-belts, hah! You're not kidding!"

Purple-red dusk was rolling down from the mountains as the airport taxi set him down by the steel-frame gates, wheeled away and went protesting back up the steep little side road. Solo stepped close, directed a long arm through the grille and around the corner to the switch that sent the gates swinging open.

There had been no hint of communication from Louise. He would have been able to feel it had there been any. The fact bothered him. He leaned on the gates to close them and began walking up the drive. That walk seemed to have no end. His nerves were on tiptoe and every shadow offered refuge for possible danger, a temptation to alarm. The biggest worry of all was that with Louise rules were elastic. She could make them, and keep to them, so long as it suited her. But she could also toss them out of the window as and when she felt like it.

She must know, by now, that he was near. For instance, she must know that he had entered the gateway. That gate could be electrified, to discourage unwanted guests from leaning on it. And you had to lean on it to move it. But there had been no jolt, so perhaps he was clear. Perhaps! On the other hand it could well be that she was playing with him. You could never be sure.

By the time he reached the stone steps and began to mount he was moist with sweat again. And that wouldn't do. Even if she lacked every other method, Louise would be able to note his tension with the naked eye.

He paused just inside the hall doorway to take a slow look around and to cool off. Everything looked unchanged and as it had been. Then he started, nervously, as a figure moved into sight and came across the floor to meet him. It was Katherine Winter. He wasn't certain what to do with his face. She looked prettier than he remembered, unexpectedly cool and wholesome in a gay cotton print. He chose a smile. She returned it with a hint of concern.

"Nathan! I—we have been worried about you. We had begun to think something must have happened when you didn't arrive five days ago. Where have you been?"

"Oh, here and there. Ran into a few snags, but nothing serious and it's all right now. How's Madame?"

Seemingly casual, he watched her closely. After all this time he still was none too sure about Katherine. She was, without doubt, a first-class cook. Louise had sworn she was nothing more. But you could never be sure. Chances were she had a hole in her head and was nothing more than one of Louise's growths. As he watched her, he saw her beaming smile fade just a trifle.

"In there," she said, stepping aside with a gesture. "She's waiting for you. Dinner will be only a few minutes."

He nodded, went on past and into the big room, paused a moment to survey the familiar luxury, then turned and closed the door after him. Outside, Katherine stood quite still for a moment, then, yielding to a sudden impulse, she kicked off her shoes, stooped to catch them up, and went in silence to the door, to press her ear close and listen.

Inside the room there was a storm-cloud silence that crackled. The aura of lethal violence was strong enough to taste. Solo swept five pairs of eyes that were like spears, and none were more daggerlike than those of the countess herself.

"You are late five days, Mr. Solo!" she stated icily. "You will explain that delay, now!"

Outside the door, Katherine gasped in surprise. Solo? But he had said his name was Summers! She listened again.

"So I'm late!" Solo grinned lightly, although he knew as surely as he knew the day of the week that there were at least four lethal weapons trained on him under the table at that moment. "You ask me to explain? Do you need it? You know where I've been, and what I've been doing!"

"Perhaps," she said silkily. "Just the same, tell me now."

"All right. I ran into trouble changing planes. In Rome. An U.N.C.L.E. agent got curious. He wasn't sure, so he started asking awkward questions. I gave him a run. It could have been fun, but I was in no position to play games, so I slipped him and found a hole to hide in. Just one of those things. All clear now. Satisfied?"

Katherine, pop-eyed and breathless, was fascinated. She had heard of U.N.C.L.E. Now she realized that these people were on the other side. *All* of them, including Mr. Summers, who was now Mr. Solo. *And* the countess. She wriggled her ear closer still, holding her breath, and heard a chesty growl.

"This is perhaps true. We heard rumors of such a disturbance, but no details, just that U.N.C.L.E. and the police were in a mix-up. Why did you not come to us for a cover, Mr. Solo?"

"This," Louise explained, "is Signor Cesar Scortia—"

"I know," Solo interrupted, grinning. "Head of Thrush-Roma. I've seen your pictures in the files. And I imagine you'd recognize me, too. So what would have happened if I had tried to solicit help from you, signor? I know that I am no longer working for U.N.C.L.E. Louise knows it. But did *you* know it?" He shifted his gaze to Louise herself, and even now he could feel the magic of her vibrant personality. She was a lovely woman, and looked as outrageously beautiful as ever. It took some effort to look her straight in the eye, but he managed it.

"You have me on a string, Louise, and I know it. You have your fun with me because I'm helpless. All right. But do you realize just how difficult it is for me? I'm known. Every U.N.C.L.E. agent knows me on sight, and so does just about everyone in Thrush. I have no friends at all. I can't afford to take chances, at all."

Incredibly, she managed to look concerned. "It is true, my dear. I had not thought. It shall be corrected at once. I will inform all Thrush centers that you are my man, from now. And I will be especially nice to you as a reward. Later. You have done well."

"Just by the way," he said, concealing his relief. "You ought to know that Miami is warm, right now. Like Paris. The fuss in Rome was because an U.N.C.L.E. agent climbed aboard and trailed me all the way from Miami. My guess is that they had suspicions, but couldn't prove anything. Just a warning of how the wind is blowing."

Halfway down one side of the table a slim brown-faced man stirred and turned his slanted Oriental eyes on Solo.

"Kow Li-Ching," he said, "of Hanoi. If the eyes of U.N.C.L.E. are so keen elsewhere, why not here also?"

"Mr. Kow!" Solo nodded politely. "Think it over a bit. How would you work a stake-out here, on a place like this? On a small island, on a house that is backed up against a mountain, with an open view of any sea-approach, and only one access road, which is barred by a steel gate. And thousands of inquisitive Corfiote eyes watching every strange face in the hope of making a drachma or two. No, sir. You have to hand it to Louise. She has this place fixed up as foolproof, believe me."

He watched the countess, saw her lingering suspicions melt away into pleasure, and once again he felt relief. Unpredictable as she was, and brilliant too, he had learned one thing, that she liked butter, the more thickly it was spread, the better she liked it. She was almost purring now as she turned a dazzling smile on him and beckoned.

"Come and sit by me, my darling. You have brought the precious things for me, haven't you? Good. You must forgive me for seeming to doubt. I was only making a test. I knew that you would not be false to me, ever."

He went to sit by her, to hand her the little packet of modules, and to pretend to be mollified. One hurdle was past, but there were plenty of hazards ahead. By far the most dangerous was Louise herself. Even though he knew exactly how fiendishly ruthless and evil she was, she was still all woman, and fascinatingly lovely. As she laid her exquisite hand on his wrist and patted it, he felt the electricity of her charm. The glittering attachments on her silver bangle were instruments of nightmare, but they hung from an arm that was a poem in shape, wreathed in skin like satin. Her silky midnight-blue gown swooped alarmingly low in front and between the magnificent swelling curves so proudly revealed lay a tiny silver key, depending on a slim chain. And that was the key to her electronic death-grip on her helpless slaves. Solo eyed it, watched the generous flesh rising and falling, and knew that he was in for a tough time and would be glad when it was all over. As Waverly had said—it seemed a long time ago—this woman was very dangerous indeed.

On the other side of the door Katherine Winter inhaled a deep and unsteady breath, her head whirling. Out of the confusion, one thing stood firm. No matter what that nice C.I.A. man had told her, she was determined to find out more. And this very night, too. There was something *very* queer going on here, and she was *not* going to sit by any longer and pretend not to notice. She was going to snoop, so there! And then, all at once, she remembered her professional duties. The dinner! Aghast, she fled for the kitchen on stockinged feet.

CHAPTER ELEVEN

THAT DINNER was a knife-edged and nerve-wracking business. Solo had to call on all his resources, to remember just how he had been before with Louise, and to play his part right, yet not to say too much, because Katherine the innocent was present. Quite unnecessarily, he was formally introduced to the other guests at the table. He could have named them offhand, from his memory of the files at U.N.C.L.E. Headquarters.

One, a large blond beast of a man, was Willy Bulow, big boss of all Thrush activities in Scandinavia. He could have won a part in any Viking movie. Another was Felix Bressant, a rat-faced elder who had most of the seamier side of Marseilles in his pocket. It was quite a gathering.

While he was playing his part, Solo was haunted by an inner vision, of Thrush satraps all over the world spreading and growing under the influence of men like these—the word passing around that Countess Louise had slaves for sale. Perfect slaves. Tailor-made androids like Adam there, who waited on them at the table as impassively as a Greek God come to life. And the hard-eyed men would come, like these, the way others had before them. And they would depart again, each with his precious slave. And each with a thing in his skull, not realizing that when the moment came, Louise would push the button and *they* would all be slaves. *Her* slaves!

He was glad when the meal came to an end, when Katherine rose and excused herself on the time-worn old plea that she had to be up and about in the morning early. She departed. The rest of them congregated in that spine-chilling room where Louise had arrayed her samples, the row of cabinets, each containing an inanimate but perfect human being, just waiting the call to stir into life and obey. Solo felt his nerves wind up as tight as piano-wire. From here on he had several things to do, and they had to be done just right, in the right order, and not one could be missed.

For a start, he stood obsequiously by the door to hold it open while the others stalked in. Then, exactly as he had gambled, Louise waved him away from the door, shut it herself and turned the key in the lock. The movement of that key shattered a tiny capsule of corrosive fluid he had inserted while standing there. Within a minute or two that lock would be useless junk, no more than an ornament. Where her secrets were concerned, Louise had an understandable passion for locked doors and no interruptions. Solo knew that. He also knew what was about to happen, if he could work it, and he had no intention of being locked in that room in that event, not if he could avoid it.

Her next move was to wave them all to be seated while she left them for a moment.

"Only into the next room," she explained, with a glittering smile. "I must prepare for the operation, you see. Also to get my instruments—and my cash-box. Napoleon, darling, you will stand by this door, and see that none interrupts."

It was all said lightly and with a smile, but there was no doubt in any mind present that Louise had not the slightest intention of trusting any one of them, except, possibly, Solo himself. She wouldn't, Solo mused, go even that far, if she hadn't been convinced that he was under her control. So, by the time she came back through that door, and locked it, it also was useless as a precaution.

In any case, the Thrush four were in no mood to notice small details. Louise had prepared herself for a spectacular, as always. She had stripped herself of all clothing, and wore only a small white apron with pockets. Under each arm she carried a small steel box. She stood a moment to meet their wide-eyed stares with a haughty lift of her chin.

"Are you all so naïve?" she demanded witheringly. "When one has a perfect body, there is nothing to be ashamed of. I am proud of mine. I do not care who sees it. Were you so well-designed, you too would be proud to show. Remember this. Perhaps, afterward, you will come to me and let me do something to correct your defects!"

Then she marched to the head of the table.

Solo stood back, grinning to himself. She had the whip hand all the way, now, and she didn't even try to be gracious. She planked the boxes down, put her hands on them and eyed the audience coldly.

"This will be done as I say, so attend carefully. I have here the sets of matched modules. You will pay me for them, now. When you pay, in turn I will present you with a pair. Then you will select the slave you wish from my collection. Then I will insert one module into the slave's brain, you will keep the other. When that is complete, then I will perform the insertion operation on each of you in turn. That way there will be no mix-ups, no confusion. Have you any questions?"

Solo had used this moment to edge gently away toward the window, which was heavily draped. Bulow grumbled an objection.

"I do not like this idea, that I am to be helpless while you do a something to my head. You so obviously do not trust us, madame. Why then should I trust you?"

"That is a perfectly fair question," she said patiently. "Always it is asked, and always I make the same reply. See"—and she spread her arms widely in deliberate exhibitionism—"I am unarmed and helpless. You are four. I operate on you one at a time. If I do something wrong to one, the others will kill me, isn't that so? So simple!"

"That's all very well," Scortia agreed. "But what about the choice? Suppose we are not satisfied with any one of these?"

"You jest, signor," she retorted. "These are twelve, all perfect, all colors, from fairest blonde to darkest brunette, and one redhead. What more do you want?"

Solo waited, tensely. He had seen this pantomime before. The Thrush men were inventing reasons to avoid the cranial operation, that's all there was to it. And Louise, in her way, was a skillful psychologist. She knew.

"You think it is not worth it, perhaps? Two hundred and fifty thousand dollars, here and now?" None of them wanted to admit that, so she pressed her point. "Very well, then. You will pay me. And then we shall see."

Bulow made it first. "All right!" he growled, and produced a thick wad of engravings of President Cleveland. "You want to count it?"

"Of course!" she said sharply, and proceeded to do

just that. This was the moment Solo had waited for. There is some unholy fascination about the sight of a large wad of banknotes being counted. All eyes were on the flying fingers of Countess Louise, none on him. He drew the drapes very quietly, eased open the window just beyond, took something from his pocket and dropped it, then closed the window again. Now he took the drapes and deliberately made a noise with them. Louise brought her head around instantly.

"What are you doing, Napoleon?"

"Warm in here," he said. "Thought I'd like a breath of air."

"Certainly not. Shut the curtains at once. If you are warm then remove some clothing. Look at me, I'm quite comfortable!"

"That's the understatement of the year." He grinned, but jerked the curtains close in time to shut out the blue glare that was beginning to show outside. "*You* may be comfortable, but it is just that which is making me warm. You don't realize—"

"Silly!" She dazzled him with a smile. "Of course I realize. You come here and stand by me while I finish counting this money. Come!"

Shrugging, he sauntered over to stand beside her. She looked up at him, still with that dazzling smile.

"Napoleon," she said, very sweetly, "I love you. You are my man and I want to be kind to you. But you must realize that I am in charge, here!" And without any warning at all she swept her free hand around and across his face with a slap like a pistol shot. It was almost as effective as a punch.

"There!" she cooed. "Now remember!" And she returned to her counting as if nothing had happened.

High on a rocky outcrop away to the south of the palace, Illya Kuryakin saw the flare and went into immediate action. Daylight survey was now about to pay off. By his side was a sturdy, rubber-powered line-thrower. He braced it now, aimed carefully by the flare, and pulled the catch. The harpoon-like rod thumped and leaped away into the gloom, trailing a fine line after it. Dropping between two crenellations on the palace roof, on impact it grew a fan of vanes that effectively jammed it as he hauled taut. Leaning on it, he made his end fast around a rock-spur.

A moment later he had mounted a tiny trolley on the bridging cable. He settled into the dangling leather straps, tried his weight, then pushed off, to go silently gliding and bobbing away into the gloom, heading for the pink and white palace facade. By the time the white wall was close the blue flare was almost directly beneath him. As he checked his flight and started lowering down, the flare sputtered out altogether. He got his feet on a balcony wall, balanced a moment, then jumped down. The stink of gunpowder was very strong. He secured the trailing ends of the hoist, drew his pistol from its waterproof holster, and advanced to the dark window on bare feet.

Katherine Winter believed far more firmly in the value of beauty sleep than ever she did in her titled employer's surgical tricks. Any other night but this she would have long ago drunk her regular nightcap of cocoa and cream, and would have been alseep within minutes. This night she hadn't even made her brew. Instead of the shortie nightdress that she preferred, as being much more comfortable than pajamas, she had chosen to climb into a jersey-knit jumpsuit, which she kept for doing her early morning setting-up exercises. Had there been anyone present to ask her, she would have said she was ready for anything that might happen.

But she was soon half-regretting her impulse to snoop, as her enthusiasm waned. Wriggling her feet into sneakers, she eyed the flashlight on the table and wished there was some honorable way in which she could just forget the whole thing and go to bed.

But she couldn't altogether dismiss the conviction that there was something queer going on. The C.I.A. gentleman had told her *not* to get herself involved, but she couldn't lean on that, not after all the talk about U.N.-C.L.E. and her discovery that all these people were on the other side.

Even the countess, she thought, standing up and seizing the flashlight. *And* that nice Mr. Summers, now Mr. Solo. He had changed, somehow. She opened her door and tiptoed out into the dark, frowning to herself over that minor mystery. He had been nice, at first. Then *she* had got at him and he had changed in some queer way, and become not nice at all. And now, somehow, he was nice again. It was so confusing! She hesitated a moment in the gloom, then set her teeth and went tiptoeing away. She knew exactly where Madame's private rooms were, and that's where it would be, if there *was* anything weird going on.

The palace, with all its nooks and passages and shadows, seemed strange and different by night. And so quiet! No matter how hard she tried to breathe quietly, her breathing seemed loud, and she was sure her heart could be heard hammering yards away. She came to the foot of a flight of stairs which led where she wanted to go.

Gulping a shaky breath, she started up. At the top she was in a dim-lit passage full of shapes and shadows. She knew quite well the shapes were only some more of the nudes Madame was so fond of, but they seemed to leer at her and grin in the gloom. She came to the door, and put her ear to it nervously—and almost died, there and then, as she heard the most hideous scream she had ever heard in all her life. It ripped the silence to shreds, turned her blood to ice water. Then came a quick snapping shot. Then the scream sounded again, followed by a boiling string of vituperation in fluid French. Katherine tottered away from the door, pressed herself to the wall and tried to melt right into it.

Illya Kuryakin heard the first scream as he was putting his hand to the catch of the window. He froze dead still. He heard the shot. On the second scream he twisted the catch, flung the window open and went through on the run, low and fast. There, backing away from the table and spitting curses, was a naked black-haired Venus clutching a wine bottle in her hand. Her curses were aimed at Solo, who had his back to the far door and on his toes, gun in hand, alert for anything. The crashing open of the window triggered off the whole spring-tight situation. Four gray-faced men around the table jerked into sudden violence. The woman hurled the bottle. Solo flung himself aside to dodge it.

That move got him out of the way of a bullet. Kow Li-Ching swung and leveled a heavy-bore pistol at Kuryakin, who snapped a shot back at the same time. The heavy-bore boomed like a cannon in the room. Kuryakin felt the breath of that bullet by his cheek, saw the Chinese lean over and sprawl, to slip from his chair. Then he went down and over in a furious roll as a shot from Scortia tore the air where he had just been. That bullet dug white splinters out of the parquet floor. Still at the table, Felix Bressant drew a careful bead on Solo, then coughed and sagged forward as Solo's shot got home first. Bulow, up and away on his feet, plunged for the door, snapping off a shot as he went. Scortia waved his gun anxiously, seeking Kuryakin, who came out from under the far end of the table and snapped a fast shot that rocked Scortia back and must have struck a nerve, for the Italian went down with his trigger-finger crooked, and the gun in his hand bellowing shot after shot until the clip was spent. Solo whirled and took off after Bulow.

Outside, Katherine molded her soft curves to the wall and prayed for sanity. The screams, shots, the uproar, all conspired to paralyze her mind, her heartbeat, her breathing. She dwindled into the shadow of a statue as the door was flung open, spilling yellow light. Out came the big blond man from Scandinavia. She saw him run for the top of the stairs. He had a gun! Mr. Summers-Solo came rushing out of the door now, and he had a gun too. The blond man heard him, spun around and fired. Solo ducked back frantically and the heavy-caliber bullet plowed into the door-frame. Solo bobbed out again, fast and in a low crouch. Skidding to one knee, he aimed and fired. Bulow stiffened, half-turned; the gun in his hand roared once more. The bullet struck the statue where Katherine cowered, making an oddly liquid "plop." The statue rocked and fell. So did Bulow, backward, in a sacklike tumble down the stairs.

Silence rushed in, seeming to echo and reverberate after the clamor. Solo climbed to his feet, dusted off his knees and sighed, then headed back into the room. Kuryakin saw him come in, through the blood-haze in his eyes. In a moment of carelessness, two steel-like hands had closed on his wind-pipe from behind, and he couldn't hold out much longer.

Squandering all his remaining energy, he heaved up, swung his arms forward, then slammed them back, elbows first, into solid flesh. The grunt of response was welcome. So was the momentary relaxation of that stranglehold.

Tearing free, gasping for breath, he spun around, raised his hand and brought it down like a hammer, with the pistol-butt where it would do most good, on Adam's bowed head. The Greek statue-man went down heavily, then started doggedly to get back up again. Kuryakin, laboring for breath, took careful aim and slammed down another hammer-blow. To his astonishment, it needed a third to put the man out for keeps.

"One of the countess' own make, I think you said, Napoleon?" he puffed. "She certainly designs them rugged. For a while there I thought he was going to tear my head off!"

"You all right now, Illya?"

"All down one side, yes." Kuryakin worked hard to catch up on his breathing while he cast a calculating look around the scene of carnage. In a moment he said, "Maybe I'm wrong, Napoleon, but I can only count up to five!"

"And all this time I thought you were a smart Russian!"

"All right, how many do you make it?"

"Eh?" Solo, suddenly alerted, ran his eye over the bodies and made a quick count. "Bulow down the stairs. Scortia. Bressant. The Yellow Peril and the android. My God, where's the lady herself, Louise?"

"Perhaps she just crawled right back into the woodwork?"

"And that isn't nearly as funny as you think, old man. If she has, we are going to have one sweet job trying to get her out. This crazy palace is stiff with secret passages."

"I suppose she's not actually here, among the assorted bodies?"

"Those, you mean?" Solo indicated the sprawled and lifeless "samples" that were scattered at all angles in the background. "Won't take a moment to check. Give me a hand and we'll stack them back in their caskets." As they labored at their grisly task, he explained what had happened.

"She started in to activate all of them against me, you know. That was a close call. I didn't know she had all of them already primed with her own modules. Of course, the ones I brought were fake, as you know. When the Thrushes had paid up, all nice and willing, and made their choices, I thought it was time to make my play, so I broke loose, went over to the door, drew on them, and she started in telling them some home truths. Naturally, she grabbed for her bangle-charms and tried to turn me off. And it didn't work. That's what made her scream, the first time. Then, like a flash, she hit a master-switch of some kind, and all these lovely ladies came promptly out of coma and started for me."

"They look—and feel—real enough," Kuryakin murmured, as they stood the last one peacefully upright in her velvet-lined box.

"They are real, so far as the physique is concerned. But just bodies. No minds. Even Adam, there, hasn't a lot of wit. Just enough to do a few routine chores. As you saw, he didn't even have enough sense to lie down when he was clobbered. That was what threw me. I couldn't have shot them down!" Solo straightened up, dusting his hands and recalling that queasy moment. "It was sheer luck that I thought of snapping a shot at that control-box of hers. And that, of course, stopped them cold. They just fell over. That's what made her scream again. She's over the edge, Illya. Jumped the tracks!"

"Not," Kuryakin said quietly, "to the extent of forgetting to take the money with her. At least, I don't see it anywhere."

"That's a point!" Solo scanned the room rapidly. "It was in a box, and that's gone too. A million bucks!"

"A nice round figure. Napoleon, you did say there is no other way of getting out of the palace, except from the front?"

"Right. That's why you had to fly in."

"Very well. She has the cash. She won't leave without it, and you can't stuff a million dollars down the front of your dress the way you do in the movies!"

"Especially the dress you don't have on. You are a smart Russian, after all. You step out onto the balcony and flash the yacht. I'll run down to the hall and put all the lights on, courtyard and everything. We're going to need help with the bodies in any case, but so long as we make sure she can't get out, we can take our own time ferreting her out. This place will have to be gone over inch by inch in any case."

CHAPTER TWELVE

KATHERINE WINTER heard this extraordinary dialogue as if in some hideous nightmare. The stricken statue had fallen sideways, pinning her to the wall. Its nude weight felt rubber somehow, not a bit the way she expected a statue to feel. Not marble. It felt alarmingly like a real body. A *dead* body. She kept quite still, not at all sure whether she would ever be able to move again. Rolling her eyes, she saw Solo hurry out of the door and go trotting busily downstairs. Her bemused brain finally delivered back to her the idea that the other man would be out on the balcony, flashing some kind of signal to that yacht they had mentioned. If she was ever going to get away, this was the moment. She concentrated, sent messages to her arms and legs, took a deep breath, then collapsed again as she heard a rustle and click from the darkness close by.

So near to her left hand that she could have reached out and touched it, the solid-seeming wall slid back to reveal a dark chasm, and then a face peered out. Just one breath earlier, Katherine would have sworn piously that life could hold nothing more terrifying than what had just happened in the past few minutes, but when she saw that face emerge and catch the light, all previous starts and shocks paled into trivia. She stared. She wanted to scream but her tongue stuck to the roof of her mouth and her throat dried into sand. If she had not already been leaning against the wall, she would have folded up on the floor.

It was Madame, the Countess Louise. And yet not. The flawless lovely features were the same, but those lovely lips were drawn back over gleaming teeth in a smile so evil and sinister that Katherine's blood ran like ice. And the eyes glittered with a light that had nothing of sanity in it at all. Deep in its throat the beautiful evil vision laughed, and it was an insane chuckle that Katherine was to remember all the days of her life, a cackle of complete insanity. The rolling, peering eyes swept the gloom, lingered for a terrifying moment on the shadows where Katherine trembled, then moved on. The head emerged further, followed by the classically perfect body, the dim light spilling over the naked curves. For some odd reason, the very perfection of that figure made the whole business seem even more horrible to the petrified watcher. She saw Louise pad away like a pale cat in the gloom, and she knew there was more evil yet to come.

She sagged back against the wall and tried to put her scrambled ideas into some sort of order. Solo, for instance, now seemed to be on the good side again, and she found a moment to be glad of that. But what had the bad ones been up to? What had Solo meant by making the bodies come alive? Surely—and chills chased themselves up and down her spine as the thought shaped itself in her mind—surely he didn't mean these statues? Could they really be made alive?

Katherine shivered, and peered with wide eyes as large men came tramping up the stairs and went back down again carrying bodies. Then she saw a slim fair-haired man in brief blue swimming-trunks come out of the door. He had a leather harness that held a gun and a flashlight. One of the other men spoke to him.

"Is it all right if we dump these in the hall downstairs, Illya? Doc Harvey wants to take a look at them before we haul them out to the yacht."

"She came ashore with you?"

"Downstairs right now, waiting."

"Women! I *told* her to stay put until everything was clear. We have enough trouble on our hands as it is. I'll go down and talk to her. We have to remember that the countess is still loose, and dangerous."

The little knot of men moved to the top of the stairs. The one named Illya paused to look down and call out.

"Napoleon, what about the cook-housekeeper? We haven't seen anything of her, and she *must* have heard the racket."

"Kate? I don't know about her, Illya. She went off to bed right after dinner. She has her own room in the West Tower. It's possible she never heard a thing. Louise reckoned to keep her night-time cocoa laced with sleepy-bye powder. But you can't believe that. She may be one of the zombies, for all I know. Either way, she won't bother us any."

"Maybe not, but she could be in danger. What if Louise grabs her as some kind of hostage . . . ?"

The voices dwindled as the men went away down and around a corner, leaving Katherine on her own. She was in a new quandary. She heaved the leaning statue away from her, then herself away from the wall, and stood on very shaky legs, trying to decide what to do next. Where to go?—with that crazy woman roaming about, and all those tough-looking men with guns! And bodies!

From somewhere came a last flicker of curiosity, sparking her to steal as far as that door and peer inside. It was quiet now, but the smell of gunsmoke was strong. She dared herself to go in, and to gape at the silent array of lovely, lifeless bodies. These were not statues. She knew that at once, by some instinct. They were real creatures, and very beautiful. She went on further, into the small room next door. It told her very little. It was full of stuff that looked like radio sets and signaling equipment. And it went nowhere. She wandered back into the main room, wondering why U.N.-C.L.E. should be so interested in all this. What had Madame done?

Then, in instant terror, she heard footsteps and voices and people returning. She had to hide. But where?

Napoleon Solo scowled, rubbed his jaw ruefully and tried to smother mounting irritation as he and Kuryakin escorted Susan Harvey up the last flight of stairs to where the carnage had taken place. For once he was inclined to share his colleague's disapproval of interfering and unreasonable women.

"Look," he said, with long-suffering patience, "I know you have a professional interest here. I appreciate that. You've seen the tanks where she used to grow the bodies. You've seen the layout. Now, you say, you want to see the finished article. All right. But please remember that we, too, have a professional stake in this. Remember, Susan, that you are not a field agent, and that we are. Remember that that woman is still loose, and that she is dangerous. Incidentally, her cook-housekeeper is loose too, and may be just as dangerous as she is.

This is no place for you. Now why don't you take yourself quietly off, back to the yacht, let us get things cleared up here—and you can examine the androids all you want—"

"Right now!" she insisted stubbornly. She had thrown on a towel-wrap over her bikini, and she plunged her hands into the pockets of it now. "I want to see the androids as they are. I want to see the control mechanism. If possible, I'd like to activate one—"

"You're out of luck," Kuryakin told her bluntly. "I took care of that. I'll show you. The switchgear is in here, for the heavy stuff. That little control-box is only a relay. I can follow it fairly easily from the diagram we had. Look, I closed this breaker, and these switches, and blew a heavy charge through the whole range."

"What did that achieve, Illya?" Solo inquired.

"This is designed to be tuned in on any or all of the modules. I set it to cover the lot, and then blew them. That means there are no longer any android slaves working for Thrush."

"Hey!" Solo was struck with sudden inspiration. "That could also mean that all the Thrushes who have bought androids have also—stopped working. Couldn't it?"

"It could. And I am not about to lose any sleep over that, either. So there it is, Dr. Harvey. There's nothing left to see."

"Was it necessary to ruin the whole thing?" she demanded angrily.

"I think so." He met her blue-eyed stare with equally blue-eyed determination. "I think this is one secret that is just as well forgotten!"

All at once she shrugged and turned away, to go back to the table and sit. "I suppose you're right, Illya.

They are beautiful." She looked at the mute line of motionless figures. "But they would pose some really terrible problems. Would they really be people, with rights and privileges, and emotions, and all the rest of it—or just property?"

"It's a tough question, all right." Solo sank wearily into the seat by her side. "I doubt if we are qualified to answer it."

"That's why I took it on myself to destroy the stuff." Kuryakin came to settle in the seat on the other side. "Slavery always is a problem, and this one—" His words cut off as a hideous cackle came from somewhere near, and by reflex he started to move. But the chrome-steel bands which clicked out of the chair were faster. With quiet strength they looped and clicked, one around his chest, one around each ankle, one around his left wrist. The right wrist, complete with pistol, was free.

He squirmed around frantically as far as he could, trying to get a line on that insane voice, a glance showing him that both Solo and Susan were totally trapped. His quest was vain.

As he wrenched himself around an empty bottle came down with crushing force on his wrist, to send the gun flying. The bottle rose and fell again, this time on his head. By the time the bells had stopped ringing in his skull, Louise had moved out and around, facing them across the table.

Kuryakin shook his head just once more, tried his bonds, and then settled for a bleak stare. So this was the famous Countess Louise! Never before had such stunning loveliness been regarded with such scant appreciation. She was totally nude, and even in her mania there was an inherent pride, a panache about the way she held herself, as if she knew that she was without flaw and good to look at.

"An animal!" Kuryakin muttered. "Madame, you do well to discard all clothing. Primitive animals have no need of it."

Something of his chill contempt seemed to strike though the fog of mania in her mind. She stiffened, glared at him, then bared her teeth in an evil leer at Solo.

"You don't think so, dear Napoleon. Do you? You loved me once!"

"Under compulsion," Solo retorted, his voice thick with revulsion. "You had a knife in my brain. It's not there now."

The lovely face contorted, swung aside to Susan. "You! Interfering busybody! Conceited, too. I have been listening. You think you are a good-looking woman, don't you? Look at me, and despair. Look at my lovely creatures and think again. And you, Mr. Kuryakin. Oh yes, I know you. I know all the U.N.C.L.E. agents by sight. Your precious organization is going to be short of three valued members when this night's work is done!"

"You'll never get away with it, Louise," Solo snapped at her. "You know there are more where we came from, that you'll be hunted—"

"Get away?" she screamed. "I do not intend to get away. Mr. Kuryakin there has called me an animal. Perhaps I am. When all I have worked for has been destroyed, do you think I care to live? Does an animal go on living when its nest has been fouled? You have come here, into my beautiful home. You have destroyed my beautiful creations, my beautiful people. Now I shall destroy you. I shall watch you die. This is something

I have long been ready for, just as I planned those trap-chairs long ago, in case of trouble."

"What are we to die of, madame?" Kuryakin needled her. "Old age?"

She cackled shrilly and backed away to stand between the two center caskets and drew aside a priceless old shawl that hung there. "Old age? I do not think so, Mr. Kuryakin. When I pull this switch, the whole of the ground floor will burst into flame." She put her hand on the red lever, and for one moment they all had the impression that she was coldly sane.

"This palace is full of treasures, things beyond price. I never intended to leave them to anyone else to pick over. I shall take them—and you—with me. So!" And she swung the lever over powerfully.

The three prisoners tensed, expecting some kind of explosion, but nothing came. They stared at the demented woman. She stared back at them, grinning. Then it came, faint but unmistakable. The smell of smoke, and fire.

"She's done it!" Solo gasped. "She's fired the place!"

"Quite right, darling Napoleon. Planted incendiary charges. The whole ground floor, and the cellars, are all ablaze by now. Pretty flames. I must see them!" She ran to the door and opened it, went out to stare down the stairwell. Kuryakin heaved desperately at his bonds, trying to make some good use of his free hand.

"You'll never do it, Illya," Solo told him grimly. "They're rugged. And remotely controlled. Louise is the crafty one, all right." He made a stiff grin for Susan, was about to frame an apology, when his eye caught the sudden stir of movement and he stared. They *all* stared as one of the "lifeless" nude figures suddenly stirred, moved, and sprang lithely down from a casket. Solo was the first to comprehend.

"Kate! You smart girl, you're a life-saver. Now, quick, find the switch for these damned shackles and get us loose before she comes back.

"Where?" she quavered, staring helplessly about. "Where do I look?"

"Back of us, somewhere," Kuryakin advised. "Try the wall. She came from that direction. . . . Too late, here she comes! Grab my gun, quickly!"

Katherine halted, dithered in confusion, then shrieked as Louise ran back into the room. One fast glance from those keen eyes was enough to take in the situation. Snarling, the countess plunged forward. Katherine, driven into frantic action, leaped for the gun, missed it, sent it skittering away into a corner. She dived after it. Louise screeched and dived after her. The pair of them went down in a furious tangle of arms and legs on the floor, where the three prisoners could see nothing of what was happened. They could only hope and pray, as they listened to the swelling roar of the flames.

The stench of burning was very strong now. They could hear the snap and crackle of vigorous flames as priceless tapestries and rare antiques caught fire and roared into destruction. Over the roar came the squeals and gasps of the two struggling contestants for the pistol. All at once came the whipcrack of a shot. A groan. Then a terrifying silence. And then a long slim arm came up over the table, bore down, and Katherine stood up, shakily, with the pistol in her hand. She stared down. With her other hand she brushed away the tangle of blonde hair from her face. She was chalk-white.

"I shot her!" she gasped. Then, more loudly: "I shot her. She's dead!" She seemed to stare at the gun in her hand as if puzzled as to how it had come there. Then she shrieked and threw it violently away.

"I've killed her!" she moaned.

CHAPTER THIRTEEN

"MISS WINTER!" Kuryakin pitched his voice to a brisk and authoritative snap. "Forget about that for the moment. It will keep. We won't. You must find the switch that controls these chairs!"

The sharp edge on his voice sliced through the frightening fog in her mind. She lifted her head, turned to look dazedly at him, and he managed a reassuring smile for her.

"Come on now, be a good girl and find those switches. Please? They must be at the back of us somewhere, on the wall."

She shivered, then went unsteadily around the table and out of their sight. Long folding ribbons of smoke began to slide in at the door. The full-throated roar of distant burning was quite distinct now. Susan coughed as a stray whiff of fumes got to her throat.

"I can't find anything!" Katherine wailed. "There isn't —I can't—oh, wait a minute. Is this it?"

Something whirred and the chrome steel bands slid swiftly back out of the way. Both men were up and on their feet rapidly and across to the door. One glance was enough.

"That's not even worth trying, Napoleon. Not worth wasting time on. You'd better get Susan out onto the balcony, quick. My tackle is still there. You should make it all right. I'll take care of Miss Winter."

Susan Harvey was a lot slower than the men in getting to her feet. Her legs weren't working very well. She had to lean on the table. She felt sick as Solo came to take her arm, and she was deathly pale. Kuryakin went straight on past him to where Katherine was straining against a wall, shaking her head as if to dislodge the thoughts in her mind.

"I killed her!" she mumbled, biting on a knuckle. "I killed her!"

"You had no choice, my dear. You did very well, and we owe you a lot. That was absolutely brilliant of you, to hide yourself among the nudes."

The word "nudes" struck home, penetrated her shocked mind, and she gasped, then cringed in a vain attempt to cover herself. Kuryakin bit back the urgent words on his tongue that this didn't matter at the moment. His common sense warned him that this was a very frightened girl, only just clinging to the thin edge of control.

He spun away, saw Solo leading Susan Harvey unsteadily toward the window. The room was beginning to fill with gray pungent smoke. He looked around anxiously, then stepped away to reach up and pluck a gorgeous Castillian shawl from the wall. Spreading it, he went back to Katherine.

"Here you are," he said quietly. "Wrap it around you. You'll need it. We're going out of the window in a moment." She stood helplessly and allowed him to drape the shawl about her body.

The room was suddenly very hot. The open window had provided a through-draft that was feeding oxygen to the fire. The parquet floor began to smolder in several places. A leaping fringe of yellow flames danced along the passage outside and leaned in at the doorway. He took her bare arm firmly and hurried her across the room to the window, out onto the balcony, shutting and securing the double windows tight behind them. Susan Harvey was peering over the balcony edge into the darkness down there.

"I can't go down!" she choked. "I can't! Not down there!"

"Oh yes, you can!" Solo told her firmly. "You just hang onto me, and you can shut your eyes if you like, but you are definitely going down!"

He settled securely into the seat harness, took her in his arms, and stepped off. The slim cable purred as it ran out. Kuryakin leaned over and out to steady it as it ran, Katherine shivering by his side and staring down in wide-eyed fright. It was a long drop down the front of the building, and the night was thick with billowing greenish fumes. Then there came a momentary break in the pall and they saw Solo touch down and roll over. They saw burly men dash forward to help. Then, all at once, that scene down there was lit up stark and clear by a gush of spouting flames from the lower windows.

Solo got free, halted just long enough to wave, then ran. Kuryakin hoisted up furiously. He felt Katherine cringe close to him, felt her shaking with fear. And he knew that her fear was justified. But now he needed her sane and steady cooperation as never before. He needed something to push her thoughts away from the danger they were in. He tried an old gambit, as he yanked at the cable with long-arm grabs.

"What's a nice girl like you doing in a low dive like this?"

She giggled almost hysterically, and then, in a much

saner voice, she said, "You'd never believe it if I told you. I mean, I haven't a badge or anything."

"Nothing to pin it on, either. What?"

"I'm C.I.A. At least, in a sort of way, I am."

"You are?" Her totally unexpected reply almost made him miss his grab on the line. "How come?"

"I suppose I'm not, not really. You see, the countess advertised for a cook-housekeeper who would do companion duties. I applied, and got the job. I really am a good cook, you know!"

"Yes, I do know." He smiled. "Napoleon told me about that part."

"And then along came this strange man, showed me his credentials and everything, said he was a colonel, I believe. He said he wanted me to write him a letter regularly, to tell him the names and descriptions of anybody who visited the countess. Just that and nothing more. He said there would be nothing dangerous about it!"

Kuryakin reached for the harness, settled himself into it, then held out his arms to her with a smile. "He was wrong on that, though, wasn't he? Come on, hold onto me."

She hesitated, suddenly shy, clutching the shawl and aware of its inadequacy. At that moment the heavy drapes on the far side of the window burst into sudden fire and flared into brilliant destruction against the glass. The window sizzled, then cracked and burst open to spout out a great bellowing blast of fire.

Katherine shrieked and hurled herself at him, clutching tightly. He grabbed hold, stepped up on the wall of the balcony and looked down as he gathered in the slack. Down there, immediately below them, a whole row of windows blasted open, exploding under the furious heat, and a raging inferno of searing flames spouted out, then licked upward with hot hungry breath.

Katherine shrieked again and clung frantically to him. He gave one more downward glance, then braced his legs and shoved off strongly, releasing the catch on the little overhead trolley. They sagged and swooped away into the darkness, safely away from the scorching heat. Which was a happy thought, had it not been for the disturbing knowledge at the back of his mind that whereas nylon is dependable and tough in almost any circumstances, heat doesn't agree with it at all and it melts rather easily.

He applied a gentle braking action to the purring trolley and felt it his duty to keep her morale up.

"You'll be a bit more careful next time you're asked to accept some commission from a strange man, won't you?"

"Never again!" she vowed. "From now on I am just a cook. Nothing else. Just for once in my life I fell for that line about my patriotic duty. Just once, I got nosy, curious, minding somebody else's business. Just once, and now look at it! Never again!"

"Don't say it like that," he chuckled. "If it hadn't been for you and your curiosity, and your quick inspiration, I hate to think where I would be right now." At that moment, from behind them, came a rolling roar and a great fountain-billow of flame as the whole of the top of the palace fell inward into ruin. Their line sagged abruptly. They plunged, then jerked as it caught on something and held. He looked down. They were only feet above the dark ground. He released the lowering line urgently and they went down, to strike and thump down into the uncertain footing of a flowerbed, and go sprawling. First up, he extended her a hand, hoisted her to her feet and put his arm around her as they stared fascinatedly at the blazing ruin. Impulsively, his arm tightened around her shoulders.

"But for you," he said, "I would be in there, frying! If the C.I.A. doesn't give you a medal for that, I will!"

She giggled unsteadily, and clung to him. Then, in breathless panic, she gasped, "My shawl! Where's my shawl?"

"Draping that rose bush," he said, and went to get it, and handed it to her. "It doesn't do you justice," he said. "I hope you don't mind, but I shall always remember you just as you are now, one of the bravest girls I've ever known."

For a moment, Katherine stood quite still, and it was odd, but she didn't mind in the least. Then she took the shawl and wrapped it around herself and smiled uncertainly.

"I don't feel a bit brave. It's just getting to me—I've nothing! Nothing at all! All my things are in the blaze!"

"That will be the least of your worries," he assured her. "I have a rich Uncle who will be only too glad to see you right. You name it, you'll have it. I want to say this, though. We agents are often criticized for being loaded with gadgetry, yet you managed to save us all with just—with just your wit and your bare—hands!"

Then he took her arm and escorted her across the flowerbeds to the front of the blazing building, to join the smoke-blackened group of agents.

"This just about wraps it up," said one, staring at the fire.

"But good!" another agreed. "Us too, if we hadn't

been quick. By the time it burns out, there won't be a thing but ashes and the walls!"

"Just as well." Solo sighed. "The kind of thing Louise was peddling is best destroyed. Come on, let's get back aboard before the whole of Corfu comes to stare."

They were an odd foursome as they gathered around the table in the big cabin of the yacht and listened to Solo making his report. His face was striped with soot and his suit was singed in several places. So was Susan's wrap. She was pale, but her eyes were alert. Katherine, her shawl clutched tightly about her, had eyes only for Illya Kuryakin, who lounged back against the cushions as calmly as if he had just returned from a moonlight swim. All around them was the subdued growl of power as the yacht sped through the sea.

"—and so the Argyr Palace, the four Thrushes, and the countess, are all a total write-off. Also all of her techniques and—er—creations."

"On the whole, Mr. Solo, I incline to think that it is just as well."

"I'll agree with that, sir. Just a point. None of this would have been possible, and we wouldn't be sitting here talking about it, if it had not been for the courageous, ingenious and very timely intervention of Miss Katherine Winter. That's the cook-housekeeper I told you about." Solo gave her a grin, and added. "She saved all our lives!"

"Indeed! May I speak to her?"

Solo passed the microphone over. Katherine gulped, stared at it.

"Mr. Waverly? That's not true, about me being courageous. I was never so frightened in all my life before!"

"That's quite all right, my dear. We all feel like that, afterward. I hope you will allow us to think of some way of showing our gratitude."

Kuryakin leaned forward suddenly and took the microphone.

"I'd like to make a suggestion, sir."

"By all means, Mr. Kuryakin. What is it?"

"Well, sir, Miss Winter confided in me that she was indirectly working for the C.I.A. I think she wanted just a taste of adventure. I think she has had that taste, and more."

"I've had all I want!" she declared feelingly, but Kuryakin shook his head at her warningly.

"On the other hand, she has certain talents that would make her a valuable member of any organization. Even ours. I imagine, if we asked her properly, she would agree to some kind of transfer."

"I don't follow you, Mr. Kuryakin!"

"What I'm getting at, sir, is that she really is an excellent cook. And you have frequently said that we lack that particular line of expertise!" The airwaves were pregnantly silent for a long while. Solo grinned.

"You really are a smart Russian!" he whispered.

"Let me speak to Miss Winter again, please." Waverly sounded thoughtful. Katherine took the microphone.

"Hello!"

"Miss Winter, are you really a very good cook?"

"I think so." She hesitated, then went on with stirring confidence. "Good enough for the Countess Anne-Marie Louise de St-Denis and all her many guests, with never any complaints. Good enough?"

"Hmm! Yes, I would think so. Miss Winter, I offer you a proposition. I will deal on your behalf with the C.I.A.

I am on fair terms with them. I will obtain you an honorable discharge. In return, will you accept a post with us, on the understanding that you will not in any way be involved in any hazard, that you will work only in our Headquarters, and that you will be responsible for the menu, with adequate staff and facilities? And a salary." He named a figure that made her gasp.

"Oh yes!" she said. "I'd love that, thank you!"

Susan Harvey watched as the two men beamed and congratulated the new recruit on her appointment. When the chatter had died down a little she said, "May I apply as the first pupil?"

"Pupil?" Katherine stared at her in wonder.

"Yes indeed. I can see that I have been using all the wrong techniques. I'm going to have to learn how to cook!"

If you have missed any full-length U.N.C.L.E. adventures starring Napoleon Solo and Illya Kuryakin, ask your newsdealer for them, or use order form on this page and the following page: